BY NICKY DRAYDEN

MINECRAFT™
THE DRAGON

MINECRAFT™
THE DRAGON

NICKY DRAYDEN

NEW YORK

Copyright © 2021 Mojang Synergies AB. All Rights Reserved. MINECRAFT and the Minecraft logo are trademarks of the Microsoft group of companies.

Published in the United States by Del Rey, an imprint of Random House, a division of Penguin Random House LLC, New York.

DEL REY is a registered trademark and the CIRCLE colophon is a trademark of Penguin Random House LLC.

Published in the United Kingdom by Del Rey UK, an imprint of Cornerstone, a division of Penguin Random House UK.

Hardback ISBN 978-0-593-35573-2
International edition ISBN 978-0-593-35903-7
Ebook ISBN 978-0-593-35574-9

Printed in the United States of America on acid-free paper

randomhousebooks.com

2 4 6 8 9 7 5 3 1

First US Edition

Book design by Elizabeth A. D. Eno

To Alex
Builder of wondrous worlds,
creator of magnificent contraptions,
your ideas and imagination
delight me
to the End and back

MINECRAFT™
THE DRAGON

CHAPTER
ONE

Zetta hid behind a cactus at the edge of the town square, waiting for the last few townspeople to finish up work and return home for supper. The shadows in the desert town of Sienna Dunes were growing long as the sun dipped low in the sky. The sand beneath Zetta's feet started to cool, and the breeze suddenly became crisp as the heat of the day drained away.

Zetta bundled up the collar of her blue tunic with one hand and kept her other hand firmly against her leather pack, which held her entire inventory of glass bottles, nether wart, and her prized brewing stand. She was the greatest potioner Sienna Dunes had. Well, she was the *only* potioner Sienna Dunes had. One day, however, she would be great, but first she needed to practice, and to practice she needed to fill these water bottles without getting caught.

In the middle of the town square stood a sandstone tower with small windows cut all the way to the top, and at the highest point hung a big brass bell to rally the townspeople in case of an emergency. In the bell tower's shadow sat the town's only well. Water was scarce and highly valued in the desert, and taking more than your fair share was frowned upon. If people saw Zetta filling her bottles up too often, they'd get suspicious and start poking around in her business. She couldn't let anyone find out she was experimenting with potions. Not yet. Especially not her father.

Zetta watched carefully as all the shop owners in the square began to pack away their outdoor displays. The grocer put away her fruit stand, carefully storing away the melons and berries and exotic apples for the next day. The owner of the slime shop bundled up his slime balls and shoved his display of slime cubes into a chest.

And on the north side of the square, right near the town hall, the bookshop vendor sighed as he flipped through the last few pages of a book, then placed it back onto a lonely bookcase. Apparently, he used to run a whole library, until the people of Sienna Dunes lost their curiosity about the world and got stuck in their ways. Now the old library was a cactus nursery. Like Sienna Dunes needed any more of those.

Finally, the square was nearly clear. Zetta ran over to the well and stood next to it, trying not to seem suspicious and failing badly. Her hands were shaky, and her eyes were darting all over the place. Carefully, she slipped her hand into her pack, pulled out a glass bottle, and uncorked it. Just as she was leaning over to fill the bottle, Zetta heard footsteps clomping in the sand, getting closer. She straightened up and shoved the bottle back into her pack, then looked to see Mayor Maxine walking right toward her.

"Another beautiful evening in Sienna Dunes," Mayor Maxine announced to no one in particular. She stood tall and dignified, and she smelled of the kind of delicate flowers that would instantly wilt under the desert's harsh sun.

"Very beautiful," Zetta quickly agreed. "I'm just sitting here, enjoying the breeze." *And definitely not trying to steal, er, borrow, um . . . take a little water to make potions in a town that doesn't think too highly of potioners.*

"And the wall is coming along nicely, if I do say so myself. I appreciate your work in the terracotta mines. It's people like you who keep this town safe." Mayor Maxine looked down at Zetta in the kind of way that said, *Why yes, I am the mayor. Thank you for noticing.*

Zetta became instantly aware of the orange terracotta dust that covered her brown skin. She felt the grit upon her eyelashes. In her coily black hair. In her socks. She inhaled so much of it during her mining shifts that she wouldn't be surprised if she one day sneezed out an entire terracotta brick.

"The wall is impressive, all right," Zetta said through clenched teeth. In truth, she thought the new wall being constructed around the town was an eyesore. But mining terracotta for the mayor's pet project had earned Zetta enough emeralds to afford a brewing stand, so she couldn't complain too much.

"Keep well, citizen," Mayor Maxine said, and then she was off with a hasty walk that was more like a horse's trot.

Zetta breathed a sigh of relief. She turned around and quickly filled her bottle. She didn't even understand what the big deal was. The well never seemed to run low. Once she'd helped her grandpa fill ten whole buckets and the water level hadn't even gone down an inch.

Zetta startled when she felt a touch on her shoulder, and she nearly fumbled the glass bottle into the well. She caught it at the last moment, then turned to see her father standing there, barrel-chested and fierce with a strange kind of charm. He was the kind of guy who crowds parted for.

"Dad! I—" Zetta's tongue suddenly felt too large in her mouth. She needed an excuse. Something quick, so he wouldn't ask too many questions about the water bottle.

The town's blacksmith had her store set up right across from the well. In the storefront window behind a "No En-chantments" sign, dozens of weapons and tools were displayed, made from both stone and iron. Zetta knew for a fact there were diamond tools, too, but those were kept locked up safe in the back.

"I was just about to check on the price of an iron pickaxe," Zetta blurted out. "I've been thinking of ways I can be more effi-cient in the mines!"

The stern look on her father's face crept into a thin smile. His eyes sparkled. "Finally getting serious about the job, eh?"

Zetta almost felt bad about how proud her father suddenly seemed of her. She was the daughter of the mining foreman, so everyone expected her to love mining and be as good at it as her father was. But mining was the last thing on Zetta's mind right now. It was pretty much always the last thing on her mind.

Zetta cleared her throat. "Um, gotta go before the shop closes. See you at supper!" Then Zetta ducked inside the blacksmith's and pretended to browse the iron pickaxes she couldn't afford. She watched through the window as her father milled about the town square, always moving, but never in a hurry.

No way would she be able to fill her bottles at the well with him out there. She could try her grandparents' farm. That came with its own risks, but Zetta didn't have much of a choice now. She waited until her father got caught up in a conversation with the mayor, then darted out of the shop and sprinted toward the south end of town.

The farm was a little oasis in what was otherwise sand and grit in the desert town of Sienna Dunes. Sugarcane stood stiff in the breeze, while the green tops of carrots swayed gently. Chickens clucked as they paced around their coop, eager for their next meal of seeds. A scarecrow made of some old fence posts, a hay bale, and a jack-o'-lantern stood guard over Papa Night's personal potato patch, which was noticeably larger than the potato patch that fed the rest of the town.

And not twenty feet away, Zetta's cousin Ashton swiped his stone hoe feverishly at the waist-high wheat shafts that had somehow managed to grow in the desert heat. He had to be nearly done with his chores by now, Zetta thought. She was running out of daylight, and she needed water. Plus now that she was here, maybe she could gather a few more ingredients for her potions.

Zetta had faith in herself that she wouldn't mess up this time. Her eyebrows had nearly grown all the way back from the disastrous explosion she'd caused during her first attempt at brewing. And now, she was pretty decent at brewing awkward potions, though the only thing they were good for was stinking up her bedroom for an entire day.

Finally, Ashton gathered up all the fallen wheat into his inventory, replanted the bare spots with seeds, then turned and headed off toward the chicken coop. Zetta breathed a sigh of relief, then kept crouched as she snuck toward the little wheat field that kept the desert town supplied with crusty bread loaves, and sometimes cakes and cookies. The familiar sand beneath her feet turned to brown soil, mushy and cool despite the beating it took from the sun.

Zetta tiptoed through the wheat until she reached the minuscule stream that served as irrigation. As Zetta knelt down next to the water, guilt started to worry her, so she reminded herself that she wouldn't take much. Just enough to fill the three bottles she needed to practice her potion of swiftness. She hoped she'd have more luck with a simpler recipe.

The potion of invisibility she'd made last night hadn't looked quite right and she'd been too nervous to test it out. Maybe the nether wart had gone bad. The stuff smelled somewhere between rotting mushrooms and a sweaty armpit, even when picked fresh, so it was hard to tell. Same for the fermented spider eyes, which Zetta kept in a chest all by themselves, since they were so awful to look at and always seemed to stare back at her.

The sugarcane Zetta needed for the swiftness potion was clear across the farm, and Ashton was right in her way, chasing a couple chickens that had escaped from the coop. It didn't take him long to lure them in with a handful of seeds, though. Ashton had a way with animals. Every pig, sheep, and chicken loved that kid. And he was especially loved by Ginger, the town's only cow. Unfortunately for Zetta, that was because Ashton was keen on giving each animal lots of love, and now he was sitting cross-legged, petting each chicken in turn and humming a little song to them.

A song that seemed to go on for an eternity.

But Zetta had to wait him out if she wanted to get the sugar. The sandstone homes of Sienna Dunes were packed so closely together that Zetta could have leaned out of her window and into one of her neighbors' to ask for a cup of sugar. Her neighbors were nice, and though they didn't have much, everyone always shared what they could. But they also gossiped like their lives depended on it, and the last thing Zetta needed was them blabbing to her father and him discovering she was messing around with magic. Then he'd have to tell the mayor, and the mayor would give her a very stern talking-to, reminding her of the importance of living a simple life, free from the distractions of things like potions and redstone and enchantments and pretty much anything interesting.

Which was kind of why the new wall bothered Zetta so much. The mayor said it was for keeping hostile mobs out, but other than husks and skeletons and the occasional pillager raid, Sienna Dunes was perfectly safe. Zetta suspected the wall wasn't so much about keeping mobs out as it was keeping people in. There were so many interesting things outside of their little town, but not many people had dared to leave it. Zetta's aunt Meryl was one of them, but Zetta barely remembered her, since she hadn't been much more than a toddler when Aunt Meryl had run off to the mountains to the north.

Finally, Zetta got an idea. Probably a bad one, but if she really was going to be Sienna Dunes' greatest potioner someday, she might as well start believing in herself right now. Instead of waiting out her cousin Ashton, she could use one of her invisibility potions to sneak past him, unseen. She took a glass bottle out of her inventory, the liquid inside shimmering a pale lavender.

It looked pretty enough, but when she uncorked the bottle, the pungent smell hit her immediately, making her gag. After a few deep breaths, she gathered her senses, pinched her nose, and gulped down the whole thing. Her entire body tingled like she was being tickled by a swarm of silverfish. Was this what magic felt like? Had her potion worked? Was she invisible?

She waved her hand in front of her face, but didn't see anything. An eerie feeling surged through her: a wobble in the pit of her stomach, like she was standing on the edge of a steep cliff.

She stood up in the wheat field, no longer shielded by the golden brown shafts. Now she could safely sneak past her cousin without risking getting caught. If he saw her, he'd tell their grandparents, and they'd tell Zetta's dad, and she'd be done for. But now she was safe. She crept her way through the wheat field, then the potatoes, and kept going until she was walking behind Ashton. How long would the potion last? Zetta wasn't sure. She was still a novice at potion making—a noob, as her cousin would say. Still, she was excited and couldn't believe this was working.

"Who's a good chicken? Who's a good little chicken?" Ashton asked as he petted the bird beneath her bright red wattle. "Salma is! Yes, she is!"

Salma clucked and flapped her wings.

"And who's the sweetest little chicken in the whole Overworld?" he cooed at the other chicken. "Nella is! She is for sure!" Nella nuzzled against Ashton's chest. "She's the sweetest—"

Ashton stopped, turned around. He looked straight at where Zetta was standing. She went as still as cobblestone and held her breath.

"Ummm . . . Cousin Zetta?" Ashton asked.

Oh no. Her cover was blown. "You can see me?" she asked, disappointed.

"Uh, yeah. Some of you. Your head." His big brown eyes were wide as saucers. "It's just kind of floating?"

"I must have rushed the brewing," Zetta mumbled. "Or I didn't use enough nether wart. Don't tell Nana and Papa I was out here, okay? Promise me?"

"I promise I won't tell . . . *if* you let me go on your next mob-hunting trip."

Zetta sighed, then made her way toward the cow pen for a bucket of milk to undo her sloppy potion. Ashton ran along behind her.

"You're too young to be out in the middle of the desert in the dark," Zetta said. "Maybe when you're older you can—"

"You've been saying that same thing since I was eight! Now I am older. I'm ready!"

"I know you think you are, but it's really dangerous out there," Zetta mumbled as she grabbed a spare bucket and opened the gate to Ginger's pen. The cow spooked as soon as Zetta entered, though, her being a disembodied head and all. Ginger ran clean across the pasture. Zetta didn't speak cow, but she was sure that Ginger's aggravated moos meant Zetta shouldn't bother making an attempt to sidle up next to the poor creature.

She looked at Ashton. He was almost a teenager now. Thin, but nearly as tall as she was. Head full of black curls and kind eyes and a fast mind. He was still naive in lots of ways, head off in fantasies, talking about poison-breathing dragons and fiery blazes and ghastly ghasts, and always sketching them in that tattered old notebook of his. Those were the imaginary creatures the adults made up to keep kids scared and too afraid to venture far from home.

Zetta didn't believe in that sort of stuff anymore, but she had to admit her cousin was getting older, so maybe it was time to start including him in her adventures with her friends. She sighed again, then handed Ashton the bucket. "Okay, get me some milk and promise not to tell Nana and Papa I was here, and I'll talk to Rift and Rayne about including you in our next outing. I can't promise they'll be happy about it, but I'll talk you up real good, okay?"

"Deal!" Ashton said.

Zetta extended her hand to seal the deal with a handshake, which of course was useless since her hand was invisible. Ashton didn't notice her gaffe, couldn't have noticed it, and he sprinted over to Ginger. He took a moment to calm the cow down, then came back a minute later with a bucketful of warm milk.

Zetta guzzled it, feeling the magic gradually drain from her veins, and then she was herself again, a hundred percent opaque all over. It'd probably be a good idea to keep some milk on hand for any future mishaps, though she was quite sure things would go more smoothly from here on out. She returned the bucket to Ashton. He was all grins, but she didn't want to push her luck and ask for a bit of sugar. The swiftness potion would have to wait another day.

"Zetta!" came Rift's voice from back near the chicken coop.

She turned and saw her best friends, twins Rift and Rayne, sauntering back from a day trip out on the hunt. Rift was dressed head to toe in green leather armor he'd crafted himself from the pelts of rabbits. His black hair stood up in spikes, which he got to stay that way by slathering on several handfuls of green slime gel each morning. An ever-present lopsided grin often meant he was up to something.

Rayne wore a simple white tunic, with a lime green scarf draped around their neck and a quiverful of arrows slung across their back. Zetta could tell that her friends had had a successful zombie hunt. She could smell the rotten husk flesh they'd collected from where she stood.

"Hey, Rift! Hi, Rayne," she shouted, then suddenly remembered her promise to her cousin. Ugh. This was going to be awkward.

Rayne pulled a couple bones from their inventory and tossed them to Ashton. "Here—for the crops," they said, before brushing their sleek black hair from their eyes. Zetta didn't understand how Rayne could be so great of a shot with a bow with that thick curtain of hair constantly obstructing their vision all the time.

"Thanks, Rayne!" Ashton said. "Zetta, are you going to ask your friends about me hunting with you, or what?" The excitement in his words caused Zetta's stomach to turn.

"Hey, kid," Zetta said in a chipper voice. Totally fake. She knew she sounded insincere, but she couldn't turn back now. "You know, I saw that a few of the torches are out over on the far side of the farm, over by the silo. Maybe you can go check them for me? Replace them if necessary. Wouldn't want any husks spawning in town."

Ashton frowned. "You're just trying to get rid of me, aren't you!"

"No, I—"

"You can't send Ashton off to the far side of the farm by himself," Rift intervened, a sly smile on his face. "What if he runs into killer rabbits out there or something? He's way too young."

Ashton perked up. "I'm old enough. I go out there all the time. I'll check on the torches. And if I do run into any killer rabbits, I've got this." He pulled out a stone sword and waggled it around. If there was one thing that got Ashton excited, it was make-believe creatures. The kid certainly had an overactive imagination, and right now, Zetta could almost see the adventure churning in his mind. "I'll be right back!" her cousin shouted.

The sun had nearly set now, and the mobs would be coming out in full force soon.

"Ashton wants to come hunt mobs with us tonight," Zetta whispered to her friends.

Rayne quirked a brow. "He's old enough, I think. I don't have a problem if he comes along this time. I'll keep him safe."

Rift nodded. "Sounds good to me."

Zetta shook her head. She'd thought her friends would put up at least a little bit of a fight. "But it's so dangerous out there. Especially after what happened to his parents . . ."

Everyone remembered what had happened to Ashton's mom and dad. They were both miners, taking long day trips toward the Great Rift, an enormous canyon that ripped through the desert like a mile-long scar. At the bottom ran a stream of burbling lava. And deep, deep down the sheer cliffs, there were exposed veins of ore—gold, iron, diamonds—tempting the brave to seek out their fortunes. Ashton's parents had gone out on that adventure, but they'd never returned. It had left a scar running through their family, one just as deep as the canyon.

"I'm back!" Ashton said, panting. That kid was ridiculously fast. Sweat glistened against his forehead. "Did you ask them?"

Zetta laid a hand on Ashton's shoulder. "I did. We all think you're still a bit too young. But soon. Really soon, okay?"

The sad look Ashton gave Zetta made her wish she really were invisible. She knew how much this had meant to him. She grimaced, watching as he trudged away, kicking aimlessly at loose pebbles in the dirt. He was mad. Disappointed. But he'd be safe here.

"Come on, let's go," Zetta said to her friends before they could make a big deal out of her lie. In Sienna Dunes, family was everything, and they knew better than to insert themselves into family business. "We've got some mobs to hunt."

CHAPTER
TWO

The three friends hopped the terracotta wall. Past it were a few torches that lit up an old wooden sign warning that they were about to cross into hostile mob territory. But Zetta wasn't afraid, not with Rayne's bow at the ready. Rift and Zetta carried stone swords as well, though they were of questionable durability. Stone was hard to come by without digging down deep past the sand, which carried the ever-present threat of a collapse. Wood was even more scarce, so anytime the friends spotted a dead bush poking out of the ground, they scavenged it for sticks, even if they had to walk a little out of their way.

It wasn't long before Zetta heard the skitter of spiders close by, several sets of red eyes peering through the dark. So creepy. So useful. Gathering potion ingredients took a lot of time and effort, but Zetta was glad her friends were here to support her because there was no way she could do this on her own.

"I got this one," Zetta said, her grip on her sword tightening in her sweaty hand. She'd killed dozens of spiders, but it never got easier. She approached it with one eye open, her arm trembling as she swiped her sword through the giant eight-legged body. The spider jumped back, unfazed by the damage it suffered, and it surged toward Zetta, fangs bared.

"Need some help?" Rayne offered, bow raised.

"No, save your arrows for the creepers," Zetta shouted back, taking another swipe at the spider and missing this time. She wished that she could say she was better at potioning than at fighting, but honestly, it was a toss-up.

The spider got too close and bit her. Ouch. Not bad—just a nip in the elbow. She was more embarrassed than hurt. Now this was a matter of pride and vengeance. She readied her sword. Rift was next to her now, his sword drawn as well.

"I can show you how it's done," Rift said, nudging Zetta out of the way.

"Nuh-uh," Zetta said, pushing back with her sore elbow. She winced. "This is my spider, and besides, weren't you the one I had to save from an armor stand last week when you were trying to use it for target practice?"

"It was a very *aggressive* armor stand," Rift said in his defense. "And it had better gear than I did."

Zetta and Rift took a swing at the spider at the exact same time. Rift made contact and the creature vanished into a puff of smoke right as Zetta's sword was about to hit it. Instead, her swipe cut straight through the air, and she continued spinning until her sword nicked Rift in his shin.

Rift fell to the ground and started hissing, grabbing his shin and rocking back and forth.

"I'm okay, I'm okay," he said.

"I'm so sorry," Zetta yelled. She stored her sword away and kneeled next to her friend. "Are you bleeding?"

"Nah, luckily your blade is dull as dirt. We really need to keep an eye out for stone so I can craft you a new one."

"Who needs hostile mobs when I've got you two?" Rayne said, coming over to look at the carnage: one badly bruised shin, two badly bruised egos.

Zetta helped Rift up. She watched closely as he took a few tender steps.

Zetta winced. "If it hurts that bad, maybe we should turn back. We can't have you hissing like that all night."

"I'm not hiss—"

They all looked around, suddenly aware just how dark it had gotten. Not four feet away stood a creeper on four petite feet, its mottled green skin already flashing brilliant white. The creeper tilted its head, looking Zetta dead in the eyes, like it was taunting her.

"Run!" Rayne said.

And Zetta tried. She really tried, but she was petrified. She'd never been this close to a creeper before, but she'd seen the destruction they caused. Craters ten feet deep and fifteen feet wide. Rift was screaming her name. He sounded far away. Had he left her standing here, or was it her panic making everything sound tinny and distant?

Before Zetta could summon another thought, Rayne bravely raised their bow and unleashed an arrow that hit the creeper square in the chest, knocking it back. Another well-placed arrow poofed the creature for good. All that remained was a pile of gunpowder. Five minutes ago, Zetta would have been thrilled to obtain this ever-elusive ingredient that she could use to make splash potions, but now she was just filled with terror.

Rayne retrieved the gunpowder and offered it to Zetta. She took it, but she couldn't look her friend in the eyes. "I nearly got us all blown up," she muttered. She imagined what could have happened if her cousin had been here, too, and a shiver ran through her.

"Not on my watch," Rayne said confidently. "Admittedly, we could work a little better together, but we're all safe. Do you have your brewing stand on you?"

Zetta nodded and patted her pack. She always kept it handy. She never knew when a potioning emergency might pop up. Plus, she didn't want to risk her dad finding it in her bedroom.

"Cool, then let's see how these splash potions you've been talking about work."

"Now? Out here?" Zetta asked.

"I know a safe place," Rift said. He led the friends farther away from town, steering clear of husks, with their dried-out skin and slow, shuffling feet that dragged through the sand. Their moans punctured the quiet of the night. Finally, after nearly an hour, the Great Rift came into view, ripping through the desert.

Zetta's heart sped up in her chest. She'd never been this far away from town, but she could tell why adventurers were so enamored with the massive ravine. It was absolutely beautiful. The sheer drop bore sand and sandstone toward the top, but it turned to gray stone beneath, and as it plunged even deeper, Zetta could just make out some light blue ore near the lava stream at the base.

"Are those diamonds?" she asked, so excited and nervous and curious that it felt like her fist was in her throat. She'd been mining terracotta for almost six months now, and had never stumbled upon anything except coal and iron. Any ore they found was rushed off to the town vault, but miners did have rights to keep the first block of ore found in a vein of at least four blocks. Zetta imagined calling "First rights" on a diamond vein. She must have gotten too caught up in the fantasy, because now Rayne was pulling her back from the cliff edge.

"Careful," Rayne said.

"Check that out," Rift shouted, pointing at the cliff face. Jutting out from the wall of the ravine was an ancient structure that looked as if it had been half swallowed by sand. The moonlight caught just right against pale sandstone adorned with terracotta. "It's a desert pyramid," he said.

"We're not going down there, are we?" Zetta asked.

"No way. Much too dark in there. Much too dangerous. But it's pretty to look at from afar, yeah?"

"Yeah," said Zetta. Mostly still at a loss for words. The ravine was an achingly tender spot for her family because it had spelled doom for Ashton's parents, but she knew that it was a source of pride for Rift's. He was named after it, in fact. This was where Rift and Rayne's parents had first met, decades ago now. One of them from Sienna Dunes, and the other from a band of nomads that traveled the desert, trading their wares. They'd set up camp on the other side. It was a tale that was way too mushy for Zetta's liking, but it helped her to feel appreciation for the beauty out here, sitting right below the pain.

The friends settled onto an outcropping at the cliff's edge, which gave them protection on three sides. Rift took out his crafting table and fashioned a quick sandstone wall to keep any other mobs from sneaking up on them. When he was done, he crafted a campfire, then Rayne tossed some raw rabbit on it. The smell of cooking meat immediately made Zetta's mouth water.

While it cooked, she set up her brewing stand. Zetta dug through her pack for ingredients, but things were sparse. She hadn't gotten the sugar for the swiftness potion. All she had were a couple of fermented spider eyes, the spider eye from their ill-fated kill from a couple hours ago, a sickly-looking carrot, a gold ingot, a whole heap of nether wart that she'd scrimped and saved for all summer, and some gunpowder, finally. Zetta was more than eager to try it out.

"I've got a rabbit's foot on me if you want to make one of those leaping potions," Rayne said, dangling a foot out for Zetta to take.

"No, no thanks," Zetta said quickly. She grimaced. As much as she loved eating rabbit, those little feet creeped her out like nothing else. She couldn't understand how people kept them for luck. After all, they hadn't been lucky for the rabbit.

"You're sure?" Rayne asked.

"A leaping potion on the edge of a giant ravine is probably a bad idea. I can make a splash potion of poison," Zetta said. It shouldn't be that hard. Most of the exciting potions required ingredients that were difficult to come by. She knew there were such rare finds in the town vault, but Mayor Maxine wouldn't allow Zetta through those enormous, piston-operated doors no matter how much she begged and pleaded. The doors were thick, made from iron blocks, and a key was required for them to open, with technology much more advanced than anything else in the town. Sometimes Zetta had dreams about those doors and what treasures were to be found on the other side of them.

So without the mayor's help, it'd taken Zetta months and months to find someone who had a blaze rod to trade so she could have Rift craft her this brewing stand. Everything she'd learned about potioning so far had been hearsay and rumors, mostly from Reed, the guy who ran the bookshop. Sometimes he spoke to her about such things, wistful for the days when his library held books with actual knowledge. Now he sold book titles such as *101 Things to Do with Sand* and *How to Raise a Happy Potted Cactus* and *101 MORE Things to Do with Sand*.

There were no written recipes for Zetta to go by, so the exact amounts and proper brewing times were all guesses on her part. Still, she was eager and willing to experiment, even if it meant her experiments tended to go a little wonky.

"Yeah, I could toss a couple poison potions at some hostile mobs and see how effective they are," Rayne offered.

"Weren't you trying something with invisibility?" asked Rift.

"If we stand close enough together, the splash potion could work on all three of us. Think of the mischief we could get into around town."

"You get into enough mischief as it is," Zetta said. Rift was a bit of a prankster, on a mission to annoy every single citizen of Sienna Dunes with his mostly harmless tricks. With the town having a population of 325, it would take a while, but he'd yet to be detected. Rift had done thirty-seven pranks so far (that Zetta knew of), things like installing a hopper under the furnace in the mess hall so that all the food disappeared into it when cooked. He'd rigged an armor stand dressed in a creeper's head to jump out of Rayne's closet. (Rayne was still a little sore about that one.) And perhaps his best one so far was rigging the pressure plate on the mayor's office door to play an annoying tune on a hidden jukebox. It took them nearly a whole day to find the source of the awful music.

Rift hadn't pranked Zetta yet, though, which kept her on edge. He'd tried a few times, but Zetta had always caught on to it. She couldn't let her guard down around him. He was brilliant, and a great friend. If only he would use his crafting skills for good . . .

"Pretty please?" Rift asked, batting his eyes at her.

"I made a few invisibility potions last night, but they have some *issues* . . ." Zetta said. She wasn't sure where she'd gone wrong, though then again, the potion had mostly worked. Maybe with a few tweaks she'd get it right this time. "But I can try again, if you promise not to prank me. Ever."

"You know I can't promise that," Rift said. "That's like asking me not to breathe. But how about I keep you supplied with red-stone for the rest of the month?"

Rift did have a nice stash of redstone that he was learning to incorporate into his crafting, and she knew how precious it was to him. A little pile of redstone dust would stretch Zetta's potions out and make the magic effects last longer. It wasn't a bad deal at all, except for the fact that Zetta would eventually come up on the wrong end of one of her friend's pranks, and from the sparkle in his eyes, she knew it was going to be a big one.

"Fine," Zetta mumbled.

Rift handed her three piles of sparkling red dust. "First install-ment. Use it on my invisibility potions."

"*My* invisibility potions," Zetta corrected him. "You just get to bask in their aura."

Rift grumbled. "Whatever, just get to brewing."

Zetta spread her ingredients out before her. Nervousness gripped her. She hadn't even gotten a regular invisibility potion done correctly, and now here she was, adding more ingredients. She pulled out the fermented spider eyes, and everyone gasped at the smell.

"It's like a rotten egg and a soggy sea pickle got into a fight," Rift said, pinching his nose.

"Do you even know what a sea pickle smells like?" Rayne asked, looking skeptical.

"No, but I've got an active imagination, unlike you," Rift bit back.

"'Overactive' is more like it," Rayne mumbled to themself.

Then the twins exchanged deep menacing scowls. The only time they ever really looked alike was when they were mad at each other.

"You get used to the smell," Zetta said, cutting through the tension and pretending to be chill about the whole situation. Pretending like she knew what she was doing. She set her three water bottles in the brewing stand, and moments later, the whole contraption started to spit and bubble. Was the water ready for the nether wart yet? Did it matter if she put it in hot versus cold? She dumped the warts in, a whole fistful, and waited. If there were any hostile mobs still lurking out there in the dark, the scent of this potion wafting through the crisp air certainly would turn them away.

Next, she broke her ingot down into gold nuggets and crafted a golden carrot. It was a bit on the flimsy side, but she hoped it would do. She tossed it into the mix as well. The blue liquid deepened in color ever so slightly, and an odd shimmer spread along the surface.

"Night vision potion," Zetta whispered, as if she hoped the twins would settle for this. Rayne seemed interested, but Rift shook his head.

"We've got torches," Rift said. "What's next?" His nose was nearly hovering over the brewing stand.

"Back up a bit," Zetta warned. "I'm not going to be responsible if the fumes turn your eyelashes into spiders."

"Can that happen?" Rift said, backing up quickly and rubbing at his eyes with his fists. He blinked rapidly, as if trying to make sure his lashes hadn't become arthropods.

Zetta smiled to herself. "*Next* ingredient," she said, aggressively ignoring her friend's concern. "Fermented spider eye." It was definitely staring at her. Definitely.

She shuddered and threw it into the potion. It sparked and fizzled, and when the hue of the liquid turned light purple, Zetta felt she was getting close. She wiped the sweat from her brow.

Next, the redstone. How much should she use? She tossed in a handful, but nothing happened. The potion just sat there, looking lackluster. If this potion didn't work, Rift would never let her hear the end of it. Maybe she'd bragged about her potioning skills a little too much. In reality, she knew next to nothing. But Rift was so good at crafting, and Rayne was so good with a bow, and Zetta just wanted to excel at something that wasn't mining terracotta.

Might as well go for it, Zetta said to herself, then tossed the rest of the redstone in. She wasn't sure if she should wait to add the gunpowder or not, but she went ahead and mixed that in, too. Immediately, the potion flashed and spat at her. She jumped back so it wouldn't land on her skin.

"Perfectly normal," she said, managing to keep the terror out of her voice. As the concoction settled, a brilliant silvery sheen shone through the glass. Zetta dared to get close. She could feel the heat radiating from the bottle without even touching it. "We just need to let it simmer for a bit now." She dusted her hands together, like she was confident in her work and not secretly afraid her whole brewing stand would explode.

"Food's done," Rayne called out, stabbing an arrow into a

beautifully roasted rabbit to remove it from the campfire. Juices trickled out and sizzled as they hit the flame.

Zetta hadn't realized how famished she was after trekking this far from home. Her stomach finally didn't feel like it was in knots. She could relax. She took a bite and savored the meat. She loved a good feast. That was one of her favorite things about Sienna Dunes—people were always celebrating something and coming together for elaborate dinners for just about any occasion.

Rabbit stew was always a hit, as was the mushroom version her dad made, loaded up with two different types of mushrooms. Baked potatoes and fresh veggies made for great fillers, but sometimes they'd get something exotic, like a bright red apple or a melon from places where lush vegetation grew.

There was a feast for the full moon, and one for the new moon. Birthdays, weddings, and holidays . . . like Founder's Day or Miner's Day or the Eve of Hostile Mobs where all the little kids made masks of ghasts or zombified piglins or creepers and then begged their neighbors for a treat. There was a huge parade and everything, with handheld floats made of paper flowers, as well as games and prizes and fireworks.

Zetta was much too old for that now, but she'd helped her cousin Ashton with his costume last year, a giant black mask of some kind of mythical dragon that was way too big for his head. He'd needed both his hands to steady it, which meant that Zetta had to tag along with him, holding his treat bag as they walked from house to house. She'd have liked to be able to say she'd avoided the temptation of sneaking treats from his bag when he wasn't paying attention, but she couldn't.

Zetta looked up at the moon. It was down to a sliver now, which meant the Eve of Hostile Mobs was just around the corner. If she was lucky, she could snag some melon and tuck it away to practice a healing potion. Assuming she could get her hands on some more gold, too, to make the melon nice and glistering. She could almost smell the potion brewing now, sweet from the melon, and not a single fermented spider eye to foul the whole thing up . . .

. . . like this potion of invisibility . . .

. . . that she'd forgotten completely about!

Zetta sat up quickly and wiped the grease from her fingers onto her tunic, then ran back over to the brewing stand. How long had she been fantasizing about food and holidays? Had the potion brewed too long? The silvery luster was completely gone now. The potion looked beyond dull, more gray than purple, and the water had boiled down substantially. This was wrong. All wrong.

"Smells awful," Rift said. "Is it ready?"

"Um, yes?" Zetta said, and when Rift raised a suspicious brow at her uncertainty, she tapped the glass with her fingertip and said, "*Definitely* ready." She grabbed one of the glass bottles and instructed her friends to huddle close. What was the worst that could happen? If the spell went horribly wrong, they'd just go milk Ginger the cow and reverse the effects. No harm, no foul, right?

Zetta raised the bottle up high, but before she could throw it, an arrow whizzed past her ear. Rayne's head whipped in the direction the arrow had come from, and almost instantly, they had their bow drawn and an arrow notched. Right beyond the hastily made sandstone wall, three scraggly skeletons gathered, staring the friends down.

The first shot had missed, but when Rift suddenly cried out in pain, Zetta knew the second one hadn't.

CHAPTER
THREE

Don't panic, Zetta said to herself. At least they weren't dealing with creepers. The friends had a chance to live through this. Not a *great* chance, but a good one. One of the skeletons brandished a bow that glowed faintly purple. Enchanted. The people of Sienna Dunes frowned upon that sort of magic, too, so she'd never seen one up close. She wished she weren't seeing one up close right now, either.

Rift punched his fist against the ground, gritting his teeth in agony. As Zetta leaned down to check on him, an arrow zipped past her, the feathers of the fletching grazing her scalp and shooting right between the two puffs she wore high on her head.

"Stay down," Rayne barked out. They notched another arrow and didn't miss. The shot hit one of the skeletons in the rib cage, knocking it back. But it recovered quickly and started firing again.

"Potion," Rift eked out. Voice trembling. He lifted a finger and pointed at the dull, half-evaporated invisibility potion next to Zetta.

Hiding from mobs was a great idea, and if Rift had had all his health and wasn't in bad shape, maybe she wouldn't be afraid of trying it, but what if it just made things worse? "I'm not great at potions!" she blurted out. "I've never even made a potion that worked properly. I don't know what this one will do. We can't risk it."

But Zetta wasn't out of ideas. She pulled Rift back behind the crafting table, and they crouched there together. Arrows thwacked the wood, over and over. She knew Rift would be mad if the skeletons broke his crafting table. Wood to make another was pretty hard to come by, but he'd probably be even madder if he was dead.

Zetta felt defeated. She was awful at potions. Awful at fighting. But there was one thing she was decent at, despite not liking it, and it gave her an idea. She pulled her trusty stone pickaxe out of her pack.

"What are you doing?" Rayne shouted, and sidestepped as an arrow nearly caught them in the shoulder. "If you're going to fight, use your sword."

"I'm not fighting them," Zetta said. "I'm going to make a distraction."

"Hurry, then. I'm running out of arrows."

She started digging through the sand with her hands, fast as she could. With sand, the risk of cave-ins was always a real threat, but she didn't have time to worry about that now. She hit sandstone and started slamming her pickaxe down against it. She dug down four more layers, hoping that was deep enough to avoid pockets of sand falling from above. Then she started mining sandstone in the direction where the skeletons were standing.

With Rayne running out of arrows, Zetta didn't even have time to leave torches to help her see. She just went by feel, forging forward until she felt she was far enough. Then she dug back toward the surface, stair-stepping and not going straight up, which was the second rule of mining. But for all her troubles, she ended up nearly suffocating on a faceful of sand anyway. She backed up, mined several stacks of sand out of the way, and then was back at it.

Finally, the night sky appeared above her, filled with starlight and that sliver of a moon. She heard arrows shooting past. When she poked her head up, she saw there were only two skeletons remaining. Slightly better odds. But with Rift incapacitated and Rayne nearly out of arrows, two skeletons was still two skeletons too many.

Zetta was ready now, her sword drawn again. "Hey!" she yelled. "You stack of bones! Over here!"

The skeleton with the enchanted bow rattled as it turned. It saw her and made a move. The other followed after shortly. Then Zetta ran. Not too fast, because she didn't want them to give up and go back after her friends. Not too slowly, because, well, arrows and all that. She zigged, left and right, hoping they wouldn't hit her. Hoping she wouldn't run into other hostile mobs. An arrow zinged past her ear.

She couldn't keep this sprint up forever, but the skeletons would never grow tired. She noticed that the skeleton with the enchanted bow was still a little ahead of the other. She carefully changed her course until the skeleton in the front was perfectly between Zetta and the skeleton in the back. Then, when the skeleton in the back shot an arrow, it struck the other skeleton's skull. The skeleton in the front turned, and though it had no eyes or brows, it somehow looked furiously at its mate and fired an arrow in retaliation.

It was a bloodbath. Or a bonebath, Zetta supposed.

Arrows flew back and forth between the two mobs, and while they were distracted, Zetta ran back toward her friends. Rayne propped Rift up under the shoulder and they made their way back toward town.

"I really wish we could have stuck around to see if the skeleton dropped that bow," Rayne said. "It had to have been enchanted with extra power."

"Sure felt like a power enchantment," Rift muttered. "Uggh."

They moved slowly, and the sun was rising before they caught the first sight of the bell tower rising high above Sienna Dunes' town square. Not a moment later, it started ringing, and this early in the morning, that could mean only one thing.

Sienna Dunes was in trouble.

CHAPTER
FOUR

The bell continued to clang, each metallic note making Zetta's heart race faster. Her cousin Ashton—was he okay? She'd thought he'd be safer at home, but now she felt foolish for making that assumption. What about her dad? She'd told him she'd be out hunting with the twins, but she hadn't mentioned how far they'd go or that they'd stay out this long. He must be worried sick about her, too.

"Can you walk any faster?" Zetta asked Rift. On a full stomach, he'd healed up steadily and should have been back to full health by now. But he didn't seem like he was in a hurry to get home.

"It's probably just a pillager patrol," Rift said. "Nothing to get excited about."

"Yeah, Captain Zayden will take care of them," Rayne said, nodding in a reassuring way.

Zetta tried to calm herself. The twins were right. The mayor had recruited Captain Zayden from the next town over a few years ago to ensure the people of Sienna Dunes stayed safe. He led a group of volunteer fighters who were more than capable of dealing with a few pillagers.

Still, the friends found themselves walking faster and faster, and by the time they reached the town wall, they were all sprinting.

The sunrise lit the whole town in a golden haze, like a sandstorm had just torn through, but it was just sandy grit kicked up by everyone rushing to fill in the gaps in the unfinished wall. No one cared about the pattern of yellow, orange, and gold terracotta anymore. They carried cobblestone, sandstone, even blocks as precious as wood, and shoved them into the gaps in the barrier. Zetta even saw people snagging blocks from their own houses to reinforce the wall. It looked like a mosaic now, a patchwork of blocks placed with no rhyme or reason.

Real fear suddenly gripped Zetta. There was no reason for everyone to be this upset over a few hostile mobs with crossbows and maybe a witch. Something else had to be going on. Something big.

Captain Zayden barked out orders, looking very official in his dark green uniform with gold pips decorating the collar. Benjamin, the slime shop owner, was his lieutenant when he wasn't busy hunting slimes in the depths of the cave system out toward the Great Rift or tending to his store. The two of them funneled all townspeople capable of fighting to strategic places around the wall.

"What's going on?" Rayne asked Captain Zayden quickly. "How can we help?"

"Illagers were spotting coming from the east. A lot of them. I've never seen a raid this big." Captain Zayden's whole body was tense, like he was counting down the seconds until he could draw his sword and be the hero the town was paying him to be. "Help with gaps in the wall, then grab a weapon. This could get interesting."

The friends all nodded, then huddled together as Captain Zayden ran off to rally up more fighters.

"What blocks do you have in your packs?" Rift asked, taking his pack off and digging through the items to find suitable building materials. He tossed out several sandstone blocks.

"Forget the wall. We need to focus on weapons," Rayne said. "Give me all your sticks. Zetta, go fetch some chicken feathers from your grandparents' farm."

Zetta didn't like being bossed around, and besides, a few arrows weren't going to help much. What this town needed was something to even out the odds. What Sienna Dunes needed was a potioner.

"I don't have time to run across town," Zetta snapped back. "If I can get some potions brewed in time, we can gain the edge. We need to go ask the mayor for some blaze rods out of the vault. Then I can brew up some strength potions."

"The mayor isn't going to agree to that," Rift said. "And even if she does, have you ever even brewed a strength potion before?"

Zetta's hackles rose, and warmth flushed her cheeks. "No, I haven't. But I've got to help out somehow. You can go build the wall if you want. Just don't come running to me for help when it crumbles." Zetta swallowed her anger. That had come out meaner than she'd intended. She knew her friends meant well, but she wished they could just believe in her as much as she believed in herself.

Zetta stormed off toward the town hall. Mayor Maxine was on the steps out front, urging the frantic townspeople who weren't fighting to come inside and hide in the town vault to stay safe. Zetta was about to ask the mayor about the blaze rods when her father ran up to her, panting.

"Zetta! There you are, thank goodness." He shoved a stack of terracotta at her. "Here, the east end of the wall still has a huge gap that needs filling. Get these placed, then come back for more. We've got maybe fifteen minutes before the raid arrives."

"I can't, Dad. I've—" Zetta bit her tongue. But she needed to tell her dad about the potions. "I've been experimenting with potions lately, and I can use some to help with the—"

"Zetta, we don't have time for magical nonsense. Focus on the wall. Mayor's orders."

"Your father's right, Zetta," Mayor Maxine said in a stern voice. It was so sharp and intimidating, Zetta sometimes wondered if it was the reason the mayor was elected in the first place. No one wanted to stand up to her. But Zetta wasn't deterred. She believed in herself, even if no one else did.

"I need blaze rods, Mayor Maxine. I'll grind them down for powder and then make strength potions for the fighters on the front lines!"

The mayor's stiff brow slid down her face into a scowl. She didn't like being challenged.

"Please, ma'am . . ." Zetta said. "I know this town doesn't like using magic, but if you just give it a chance, you'll see how much of a difference it can make."

The mayor's brow softened ever so slightly, and she exchanged a meaningful glance with Zetta's father that Zetta couldn't understand. "You have your orders, Zetta," the mayor said, then turned away.

"*Magical nonsense*," Zetta said under her breath. Where her father and the mayor saw frivolous wastes of time, Zetta saw an opportunity. But for some reason, they wouldn't take it.

Zetta's father left the stack of sixty-four terracotta blocks at her feet, too disappointed to even look at his daughter. He ran off toward the north wall. Zetta took the terracotta and headed east. The gap in the wall here was indeed large. She started placing blocks, three high, working as fast as her hands would go. Her heart was full of anger, which only made her work faster.

Harsh trumpeting sounded in the distance. Zetta scrambled up to the top of the wall and squinted through the vast stretch of rolling desert hills where glittering mirages reflected off the hot sand. A gray flag appeared from behind a hill, not five hundred feet from where she was standing. The raid was huge. Eight, nine, ten . . . she kept counting, higher and higher. Nineteen, twenty . . . Some of the raiders had axes, others had crossbows, and there were a few witches among them, too.

And then Zetta saw something that nearly made her lose her balance on the wall. Actually, she'd felt it before she saw it, a thundering that traveled through the soles of her feet and shook

all the way up to her molars. The stomping was from an enormous four-legged beast with a thick ash gray hide, chained armor,
and horns that looked like they were made for ramming through
tough materials. Zetta had never heard of anything like it.

The last blocks were going into the wall right below her.
They'd finished the wall in time, but somehow Zetta knew it
would not be enough. Not even close.

Zetta hopped off the wall and ran back to the mayor.

"Mayor! Mayor, you have to reconsider. They've got this beast!
There's still time for me to brew the strength potions." Maybe.
The raid was so close. The thundering steps made the ground
rumble even more. Bits of rocks and pebbles jumped around at
Zetta's feet.

"I've heard. We're sure the wall will hold. We've tested it. It'll
hold." The way Mayor Maxine repeated herself made Zetta wonder if she was trying to convince herself of this lie as well.

"Why won't you just let me do this? Why won't anyone even
consider using magic?"

The mayor frowned. "Maybe that's a question you should ask
your father."

Zetta's eyes went wide. Why ask her father? Wasn't the mayor
in charge of Sienna Dunes? She was about to inquire further with
the mayor, but then an enormous thump hit the east wall. The
entire town stood still, watching as the wall thumped again, like
an enormous fist was knocking, wanting in.

"Please hold," Zetta mumbled to herself.

Another thump. This time, a few cracks appeared in the wall.

"The wall's being breached!" shouted Captain Zayden. He shook his head, like he couldn't believe what he was seeing. "I don't get it. There're never this many illagers. We've got vindicators with axes up in the front and pillagers with crossbows holding position behind them. And that beast—" He started routing his fighters to the weakening spot. After another loud thud, the air was suddenly filled with a cloud of terracotta dust, obscuring the true extent of the damage. Seconds later, Zetta heard the nasaly grunting of illagers and the clash of weapons as the raiders spilled through the gaping hole in the wall. People were screaming, running in all directions, trying to avoid the rubble from the destroyed blocks. Arrows flew.

As Zetta watched the carnage, her fingers twitched. She wished her brewing stand was warming up right now. She saw so many ways she could be helpful. Healing the wounded. Boosting speed. Giving fighters the ability to leap out of the way of danger and confuse the enemy.

"Haarrrrr!" yelled one of the pillagers. Wait, pillagers were the ones with the crossbows, right? Maybe this was a vindicator? Zetta wasn't a hundred percent sure what all these different types of illagers were called. She only knew she didn't want them busting up her town. The raider was standing not five feet in front of Zetta. She'd been so busy dreaming up potions that she hadn't noticed it creeping up on her. And now it stood there, brandishing an axe, swinging it right at her.

An arrow zinged over her shoulder and hit the raider in the chest. Another arrow followed in short succession, and the enemy died right in front of her, leaving nothing behind but a puff of smoke. Zetta looked back and saw Rayne standing in the window of the bell tower, their bow drawn and notched, moving on to the next target already.

Zetta's heart dropped to her feet, too heavy with gratitude. She should have been more supportive of her friend. But though she may have failed Rayne before, she could do better now. She ran around collecting missed arrows, and then rushed up the creaky ladder to the top of the bell tower to return them to Rayne so their supply would dwindle a little more slowly. She was on her second trip, bending down and struggling to pry up an arrow wedged in sandstone, until finally it popped loose. When she stood up, Zetta was suddenly face-to-face with Captain Zayden.

"Your friend is a great shot. Give them this," he said, passing Zetta a bow gleaming purple all over.

"Is this—"

"Enchanted," Captain Zayden said quickly. "Infinite arrows and a bit of extra punch."

"But the mayor—" Zetta started.

"Let me worry about the mayor when we're on the other side of this battle," Captain Zayden said.

Zetta stared at the captain, her jaw hanging open. She knew he could get in trouble for this. The mayor really didn't like any sort of magic being used, but Captain Zayden wasn't from Sienna Dunes, and he didn't hold their weird distaste for magic.

Zetta nodded, knowing that Rayne would be so excited to have this bow. She started making her way back to the bell tower so she could deliver it to her friend.

But as she crossed the battlefield, it became more and more apparent that the people of Sienna Dunes were peaceful folk, not fighters. Gloriana, the young woman who worked the grocery shop, was hurling carrots and apples at a couple of pillagers as she dodged their arrows. Milo, one of the town's best miners, was swinging at a witch with his bulky iron pickaxe. They were all ill-prepared and outmatched.

Even though the illagers were fewer in number, they seemed to be gaining the advantage, tearing through the town. And every time the townspeople banded together to fight the hostile mobs, the armored beast would charge at them, causing the fighters to scramble out of the way.

The illagers destroyed everything they could get their hands on, and pocketed anything of value that wasn't tied down. The vault held the town's most precious resources, though. Zetta was glad about that. Hopefully the illagers didn't have the knowledge or the patience to figure out how to operate a key-coded piston door.

Before Zetta could make it to the tower to give the bow to Rayne, the armored beast rammed through the front wall of the former library, destroying dozens and dozens of potted baby cacti. It demolished the bins in the compost center, then headed south toward the farm. Zetta winced, watching as it stomped through her grandparents' wheat field. They needed that food. That wheat was the one precious thing they hadn't stored away in the vault. They barely had enough to go around, let alone for a stockpile.

Zetta had to do something to save their farm. No way was she going to get close to those horns, but she did have an enchanted bow. She'd never used a bow before, but she'd seen Rayne shoot hundreds of times. How difficult could it be? The beast was almost too big a target to miss.

She notched an arrow and pulled back the string as tight as she could. Then she released. Somehow, though, she was left holding the arrow and not the bow, which flew straight forward, hitting the beast square in the forehead. The beast looked up at Zetta, annoyed. It snuffed its wide, flaring nostrils, then started trotting for her, a heavy hoof slamming down on the enchanted bow and smashing it to pieces.

Zetta gritted her teeth. Rayne would never forgive her for this.

But at least the beast had lost interest in stomping the wheat field, since it was now focused strictly on Zetta, and was charging right at her.

She shrieked. Rayne sunk a few arrows into the beast, but it didn't seem remotely fazed. Only its pride was hurt, from being smacked in the face with a sparkly purple bow.

Zetta ran away as fast as she could toward the town square. She looked back, making sure she was putting some distance between her and the beast. Normally, she'd be able to outrun it, but there were so many obstacles that she had to go through and so much debris to dodge, while the beast just plowed through it all.

When Zetta faced forward again, she saw Mayor Maxine

standing right in front of her, arms outstretched to brace for Zetta's impact. Zetta couldn't stop fast enough and ran right into the mayor, bowling her over. Thunder rumbled the ground as the beast came nearer. The mayor jumped back up to her feet and started running, and the beast cut away from Zetta to focus on Mayor Maxine.

Oh no. The mayor was not so fast. The beast bore down on her, taking arrow after arrow without a single flinch. Zetta grabbed her pack, which had fallen off during the collision, and reached in for her splash potion of invisibility. She didn't know if it would work, but she didn't have much of a choice now, did she? A few more seconds and Sienna Dunes would be short a mayor.

She lobbed the potion toward Mayor Maxine and hoped for the best.

The glass flew through the air in a high arc, then collided with the mayor's shoulder. She let out an "Oof" on the impact, and then was surrounded by a fog of magical particles. Something was happening, at least. The fog near the ground dissipated, and Zetta no longer saw the mayor's feet.

She'd done it! But as the fog continued to clear, Zetta cringed as she saw that Mayor Maxine's top half was still there, though it was minus a head. The beast spooked at the sight, then cut clean away, eventually disappearing back through the hole in the east wall with the squeal of a panicked pig.

Zetta's magic had evened out the odds, just not in the way she was hoping. But without their most powerful weapon, the remaining illagers were picked off by the townspeople.

They'd done it! They'd defended their town from the raid. But their win had come at a cost. It would take weeks to clean up from this destruction. Who knew if lives were lost as well. Everything was dusty and everyone was heavy with grief.

"What did you do to me?" the mayor yelled at Zetta. She looked angry, still intimidating, and somehow scowling with just two arms and a torso.

"I—I—" Zetta stammered. She was pretty sure she'd saved the mayor's life and driven a three-ton killer from their town, but Zetta felt like saying that would be the wrong answer. "I don't know, but I can fix it!"

She scurried off to the farm and grabbed a bucket and looked around the cow pasture. Her cousin Ashton was sitting off in the corner, a large slab of beef cradled in his lap.

"Ginger?" A lump stuck in Zetta's throat as she said the cow's name. Ashton looked up at her with tears in his eyes, lip quivering. The town's only cow. Which meant no more milk to reverse the potion, and that the mayor would be stuck half invisible until the magic wore off. But Zetta wasn't worried about that right now. She sat down next to her little cousin and placed a hand around his back and hugged him. "I'm so sorry."

"She was such a good cow," Ashton mumbled.

The illagers had scared Zetta earlier, but something snapped inside her. Now she wanted revenge. They'd crushed her cousin's heart by killing his cow; they'd destroyed her town. They would pay. Zetta vowed to learn everything there was to learn about potioning and to use it to her advantage.

"Zetta, thank goodness, there you are!" her father said as he ran up to her. "Are you hurt?"

"No, I'm okay," she said. "Ashton's okay, too."

"She saved us from the ravager," Rayne said, running up, bow packed away. If Rayne could let their guard down and pack up their bow, then everyone was truly safe. For now. "She's a hero!"

"She's a menace! A troublemaker," came the mayor's voice. Screams erupted from wherever her headless torso passed. "Look what she did to me!"

Zetta's dad stumbled back, unsure of what he was looking at. "Mayor Maxine? Is that you?"

"Zetta, you said you could fix this," the mayor said. "Now fix it!"

"You just need to drink some milk," Zetta mumbled, clutching the bucket to her chest. The mayor grabbed it and went to gulp it down, but it was empty. Zetta felt Mayor Maxine's invisible yet fiery eyes staring at her. "There's no milk, though. Our only cow was killed in the attack."

"So how long will I stay like this?" the mayor demanded.

"I don't know, ma'am," Zetta said sheepishly.

"This is why we don't mess with magic," her father said. "Nothing but nonsense and false hope."

"But Dad, what if the illagers attack again? If I practice and get better, then I know I'll be able to help. Please!"

"Leave the worries of defending this town to the grown-ups," Father said, puffing out his chest. "We'll rebuild the wall, thicker this time. Potions have no place in Sienna Dunes. I told my sister the same thing a thousand times over, and look what happened to her! Rotted her brain. Now all she thinks about is nether weed and glow rocks and magma sauce, secluded up in that mountain in that hovel of hers. I lost her to magic. I won't let the same thing happen to you." Father put out his hand. "Give me your brewing stand. I know you have one."

Zetta did not want to disobey her father, especially in front of so many onlookers. They'd drawn a crowd, whispers coiling through it, about how Zetta was a hero. About how she was a menace. No one knew what to believe. She handed over the brewing stand.

"Do you even know how dangerous blaze powder is?" Father asked, shaking his head. "You could have caused an explosion!"

Zetta shrugged, rubbing her eyebrow. It had been singed stubble for so long—a very awkward reminder of blaze powder's explosive punch. That's why it was such an excellent fuel source for making potions and for crafting fireworks for holiday celebrations. But there was just a handful of it inside the brewing stand, not enough to cause too much damage.

"Everyone stop staring and start cleaning!" the mayor demanded, breaking the strained silence that filled the now cowless cow pasture. Then Mayor Maxine stuck both her hands high up in the air and screamed, "And someone go find me some milk!"

Zetta shuffled back home, down but not defeated. A thicker wall wouldn't help. Why was her father so dead set on doing the thing that didn't work? Sienna Dunes may have given up on Zetta, but she hadn't given up on her town. This was where she grew up. Where her friends and family were. And she vowed to protect it the best she could.

Her father had mentioned her aunt Meryl, his sister. Zetta barely remembered her. She'd left the town soon after Zetta's mother had gotten a sickness and withered away. Zetta hadn't known she had a potioner in her own family. Maybe she could get some instruction from her aunt. She had to try.

There was only one mountain her father could have been talking about. Zetta looked out of her bedroom window, where she could just barely make out the faint top of the distant mountain peaking over the terracotta wall.

Zetta scribbled a vague note to her father, then rummaged through her home, packing up food for her journey. In the hall closet sat a dusty chest filled with odds and ends. From it, Zetta grabbed a blank notebook, its leather old and cracked. The notebook had probably been her mother's and would be great to hold all the potion knowledge that her aunt would teach her.

A pair of comfortable, well-worn boots also sat inside the chest, so Zetta snatched those, too. They would provide a little armor protection from the hostile mobs that lurked beyond the desert. She'd heard that the zombies were greener and fleshier than the husks she was used to dealing with, and who knew what other untold dangers awaited her?

Zetta shook her head to clear the worry from her mind. No time for fear. She had a long journey in front of her, a tall mountain to climb, and a town to save.

CHAPTER
FIVE

When Zetta scraped her shin for the fifth time as she scaled the steep cliffs of this lush green mountain, she started second-guessing her decision to stray so far from home. She'd tried to keep her morale up throughout her journey. It had taken her a couple hours to trudge through the desert, where the hostile mobs were familiar at least, even if they were keen on killing her.

Once she had grass under her feet, everything had changed. She'd never been farther than the badlands in her whole life. While the desert was mostly uninterrupted horizon where she could see creepers and husks from a mile off, here there were bushes and trees for the baddies to hide behind. Zetta kept on her toes, walking as fast as she could.

She stumbled upon the most beautiful flower field that took her breath away, with these gentle little insects that buzzed from flower to flower. Bees, she slowly remembered. And bees made honey. Their little pollen-covered bottoms were so cute, and they seemed so happy. Zetta picked a flower and offered it to one of the bees.

The bee buzzed up right next to her and suckled from the flower! Then Zetta followed the bees back to their home. When she was close, she caught the scent of the most delicious-smelling golden liquid—honey—just dripping from the little holes in the little insect house. Zetta's mouth watered as she collected some honey in one of her empty bottles.

Big mistake.

The gentle bees instantly became furious. Their eyes glowed red now, and suddenly Zetta remembered something else she'd forgotten about bees. They stung.

Two of the bees sunk their stingers into Zetta, and she cried out in pain. She ran away and tried to soothe the pain in the cold of a deep stream. Fish swam past her, tickling at her toes. Zetta was glad to get at least a moment's rest and calm. She could see the whole shore, and no mobs would be able to sneak up on her.

But then that gentle tickle on her toes turned into a sharp pain in her thigh. She looked under the water's surface and saw that some kind of underwater zombie was after her. A super- soggy version of a husk.

She swam to shore as quickly as she could, then looked down at the damage. Nothing a healing potion couldn't mend—but she didn't have a healing potion. She didn't even have a brewing stand anymore. Zetta had been so mad at her father that she'd gotten out of the house as quickly as possible, leaving him a short note saying she'd be back when she was better equipped to help their people. Could be weeks. Could be months. Who knew? She'd learn everything she could from her aunt and come back with a full knowledge of potioning, or die trying. Now, with the stings and the scraped shins and the zombie bite, Zetta wasn't sure it wouldn't be the latter.

She scoured the mountain, but the huge trees all looked the same, and the terrain was often impassable. Zetta couldn't see any signs of her aunt or her home. After a while, Zetta had to admit that she might not ever find her, and that this mission was a waste of time. She sat down and started to sob. Big warm tears ran down her cheeks, so many more than had ever come from her eyes. They were even running down her arms, neck . . . forehead?

Zetta touched her brow, then looked up into the sky. It was rain! Actual rain! She'd never seen such a thing. She jumped to her feet and twirled around with her mouth open, catching drops on her tongue. This was such an amazing feeling. Zetta watched the leaves jump each time drops landed upon them. Little puddles formed under her feet. In the desert, water was life, and here there was just so much of it. This was worth it. Even if she never found her aunt's home, Zetta would remember this moment forever.

When the clouds parted and the sun struck through the canopy, Zetta caught a glimpse of something. A house! That had to be it. It was quaint, but tidy, made of dark wood and cobblestone, with window boxes full of flowers and a small garden brimming with carrots, sugarcane, and melons! Rabbits roamed behind the gated fence, and under a raised porch in front of the house, nether wart grew in dark sand.

"Aunty Meryl!" Zetta yelled. Her aunt probably wasn't used to visitors, and Zetta wanted to make sure she didn't end up getting a potion of poison lobbed at her for trespassing. "Aunt Meryl, it's me, Zetta. Carl's daughter."

Nothing happened.

The rabbits scrambled away from her as she got closer. She caught a whiff of fermented spider eye coming from the house. Zetta looked up into a cobweb-filled window and could make out a set of four brewing stands bubbling together. Each potion was a different color, and storage chests were piled up along the walls, labeled with signs: blaze powder, phantom membranes, magma cream.

Zetta could hardly contain her excitement. There was so much to learn! She was about to reach into her pack to pull out the notebook, but a firm hand slammed down on her shoulder and spun her around with great force. She looked up into the face of her aunt, the brown of her skin deeper than that of Zetta and her father, hair in a giant white puff with a few remaining strands of black here and there. The resemblance to Zetta's father was uncanny, even though she was nearly fifteen years older. Apparently, the genes in her family were strong.

Zetta hoped the familial bonds were strong, too, because if she got poofed by her own aunt, Zetta would be awfully cross. And awfully dead.

Her aunt said nothing—her angry scowl did all the talking. She wore a long gray dress that looked like it had once been blue or purple, but those colors had long ago been washed out of existence. Chunks of glowstone hung from a gold chain around her neck. She smelled . . . *natural,* was the closest Zetta could come to thinking of it. Like dirt and wet leaves and moss.

"Aunty Meryl? I'm—"

"I heard who you said you were. You found your way up here, so I'm assuming you're capable of finding your way back down. Better hurry before night catches you." Aunt Meryl let go of Zetta's shoulder, but Zetta could still feel the pressure of her handprint and the bruise blooming. Aunt Meryl turned her back to Zetta, the long hem of her rough dress brushing against the earth.

"You can't send me away," Zetta said desperately. "I need you to teach me about potioning! Our town was attacked by a huge mob of illagers. Dozens of them. And you know raids come back bigger and stronger. If I knew more about how brewing worked, I could give us the advantage we need to drive them away for good."

Aunt Meryl turned around slowly. "Illagers . . ." she mumbled.

Zetta nodded so hard, she thought her head would fall off. She had to do whatever she could to get her aunt on her side. "I've been practicing! I'm not a total noob. But there's so much I don't know. I've been getting things wrong. A lot. But one of my potions saved our mayor from getting run down by this huge beast with horns."

"A ravager," Aunt Meryl said. Her voice was ragged, like she barely ever used it. "That's bold of the illagers to attack a town of that size. They usually stick to small villages filled with people who they know won't fight back. The right potions could help fend them off, but unless your father has had a miraculous change of heart, he would never be okay with such a thing. He'd rather cut off his own nose than to have another alchemist in his house. I take it he doesn't know you're here."

Zetta shrugged. "I left him a note that I'd be back when I was ready to help our town out however I could. I didn't tell him I was coming here."

"Oh, he'll figure it out. Last thing I need is my brother show-ing up on my porch demanding I stop corrupting his daughter with magical nonsense." Aunt Meryl shuddered, her face still stern, but Zetta could tell by the slight slope in her shoulders that something in her heart had gone soft. "You can stay one night. I won't teach you about potions, but I will brew you some to take back with you. If your father asks where you got them from, say you made them yourself. Never speak my name. For both our sakes."

Zetta uttered a noncommittal "Okay," still unsure what all the fuss was about. Some sort of sibling feud that thirteen years of separation hadn't resolved. She got the feeling that thirteen more years wouldn't help the situation much either.

Zetta followed her aunt inside her quaint home. Every corner of it was stacked with old chests, and the scent of fermented spi-der eyes was ever present, though the dried flowers hanging all around covered the scent up some. Several cauldrons were filled with murky-looking water, and cobwebs had settled in the nooks and crannies between the many odds and ends that probably hadn't been dusted in over a decade.

"Don't touch anything," Aunt Meryl commanded.

Zetta practically folded into herself, trying to become smaller so that she wouldn't accidentally brush against a barrel or knock over a chest filled with glass bottles. Her eyes were wide. She'd never seen such a collection of items from all over the world. In the desert, it was all sand and sandstone. And cactus. Always cactus.

The little bit of color the people had in Sienna Dunes came from cactus dye. Green clothes, green leather armor, green beds, green glass. Green fireworks during holiday celebrations. Once, as a prank, Rift had even dyed all the sheep on Nana and Papa's farm green. Zetta's grandparents weren't amused. Neither were the sheep.

But here, everything was a different color of the rainbow. Zetta could never have even dreamed of a place so beautiful and charming. The wooden floor planks were the most stunning shade of teal blue. In the middle of the room, the four brewing stands sat on a workbench made of lavender-colored blocks etched with smaller squares. Behind them, lining the far wall, was a stretch of black blocks dripping a glowing purple ooze. It almost looked like the blocks were crying. Creepy. But also pretty, in a weird sort of way. On top of them sat two large chests.

Aunt Meryl opened the chest on the left. It creaked wearily before spilling out a golden light that lit up the entire room. Zetta dared to get closer, and when she peeked inside, she saw the chest was filled to the brim with blaze powder. She could feel the heat radiating off it.

The powder spat and sizzled angrily as Aunt Meryl took a big scoopful and set it carefully on her workbench. She then stacked a pile of sugar next to it, along with some glistering melons that made Zetta's mouth water. She knew better than to eat them, since they'd been crafted with a bunch of gold nuggets, but they looked so sweet and juicy.

Zetta stayed as close to her aunt as she could without risking tripping over her or interrupting her process as she continued to gather up ingredients stored in various places. When Aunt Meryl approached an old barrel sitting under a cobweb-covered window, she shot Zetta a warning glare not to come any closer. This only stoked Zetta's curiosity. She wanted to know what was in that barrel more than anything. With a very delicate touch, Aunt Meryl reached in and pulled out a small tear-shaped object. It shone like a jewel.

Only when she had laid it carefully on a workbench all of its own did Aunt Meryl dare to breathe again.

"What is that?" Zetta whispered.

"Ghast tear," Aunt Meryl said. "Very difficult to collect. Very fragile as well, but I can make you a few splash regeneration potions that you can use if you get in a pinch."

Zetta was speechless. This was going so well. Beyond her wildest imagination. Then she watched as her aunt began to brew. In no time the room became humid, as the four bubbling brewing stands puffed steam into the air, each working on a separate set of potions. Healing, strength, swiftness, and regeneration. Zetta took out her notebook and began jotting down what Aunt Meryl was doing, trying to estimate measurements and timings.

So many questions ran through Zetta's head, but she didn't have the nerve to ask them. She could spend a year here, just watching her aunt work like this. The way she moved was almost like she was making music, and Zetta didn't want to throw off her rhythm, but finally, the words just shot out. "How do you know how to do all of this?"

Aunt Meryl was silent for a long time, as the smoke from the healing potion wafted toward Zetta. Finally, looking satisfied, she turned the burners off and set the potions to the side so they could cool. "Curiosity, mostly. Observation. Patience."

Zetta waited for her aunt to elaborate, but she didn't. The regeneration potions finished next—such a curious shade of purple. Then the strength potion—thick and dark, like blood. The swiftness potion came off the burners last, which caught Zetta by surprise. Then again, maybe that made sense. Speed took time. She jotted that down in her notebook.

Not that any of this really mattered. Her father had taken her brewing stand. Their town was in shambles. Any free time she had would be spent picking up the pieces from the raid. Zetta loved Sienna Dunes. She loved her community, but a small pit of anger prickled in her heart like cactus quills. If she hadn't used that potion on the mayor, things would have been a lot, lot worse. And no one wanted to admit it. Especially not her father.

"Why does Dad distrust magic so much?" Zetta squeaked out as her aunt was putting the corks in the potion bottles.

Aunt Meryl's hard demeanor softened significantly and suddenly. She sighed, then patted a spot on her workbench. Zetta walked over and scrambled up and sat on it, her legs dangling like she was a kid.

"You remind me of myself when I was your age. You said you saved the mayor with a potion? Tell me about it."

Zetta's eyebrows arched. No one had ever shown much interest in her potions. Rift and Rayne tolerated her rantings out of kindness, but she always felt she had to rein in the true extent of her passion so she wouldn't bore them to tears. But now, she saw how her aunt was ready to listen. Really listen. And everything she'd been holding back tumbled out of her mouth.

"It was a splash invisibility potion. But I didn't know how much redstone to use, and I think I added too much, and my golden carrot wasn't the freshest, and I got distracted and left it on the burner too long." Zetta came up for a breath, then continued, describing what had happened during the raid, and how she'd turned the mayor mostly invisible, except her torso and arms, and how the sight had freaked the ravager out.

Aunt Meryl nodded kindly throughout the entire retelling, then looked Zetta right in her eyes, so deeply, Zetta could feel it in her soul. "Alchemy is an art, but it's also a science. It requires both creativity and rigor. And if there's one thing you can't be, it's distracted. Seconds can separate a perfect potion from a disaster."

Zetta went to write that down in her notebook, but Meryl shook her head. "You haven't found any written records of potion recipes because they are not something that can be written down. Magic doesn't want to be completely known, and it changes over time. Our world changes over time, bringing with it new opportunities for discovery if you keep an open mind. There weren't always invisibility potions, you know. There weren't always pillager raids, for that matter. It is our job to learn and adapt. To discover new blocks, new biomes, new ways of looking at the world. The magic is out there waiting. You just have to find it. That's where the art comes in. Listening, observing . . ."

"Patience," Zetta said, though she was pretty sure she didn't even have an ounce of it. But she'd definitely noticed that her aunt had changed the subject away from her father and his distaste for magic. "Well then, how do I learn the art?" Zetta asked. She already knew the answer to this. And Aunt Meryl knew that she knew—that was written clearly in the hesitation on her aunt's face.

"An apprenticeship," Aunt Meryl muttered.

Zetta perked up. "Does this mean you will—"

"No," Aunt Meryl said, cutting her off. "I can't. Your father would never forgive me. But perhaps if I went around the house, muttering things here and there about alchemy . . . and if you happened to be behind me listening . . . Well, there's not much for him to be mad about in that, is there?"

Zetta nodded, agreeing wholeheartedly. "I'd like that. I'd like it a lot!"

"It's only for a couple days. He'll be heading this way sooner or later, and we'll need to have you gone before that happens. I can't promise you'll learn much, but I can at least get you pointed in the right direction. We'll do what we can to protect your home." The way the word "home" came out of Aunt Meryl's mouth made it sound like such an abstract concept, like she'd distanced herself from Sienna Dunes for so long, she'd never be able to return. Whatever rift there was between Father and Aunt Meryl, Zetta hoped they'd be able to heal it eventually.

They started early the next morning, as Aunt Meryl set a bowl of stew in front of Zetta.

"First rule of alchemy: Never brew on an empty stomach," Aunt Meryl said, stirring her own steaming bowl.

Zetta gulped, looking at the murky liquid and the colorful flecks bobbing on its surface. It looked a little . . . suspicious. "Ummm . . . do you have anything else to eat?" Zetta asked sheepishly. Aunt Meryl sighed, then fetched a pumpkin pie from a chest and dropped it in front of Zetta. Zetta's eyes lit up, and she stuffed the whole thing into her mouth. Crust crumbs tumbled out either side.

"We should do cake for lunch," Zetta said with a smile.

Aunt Meryl frowned. "Cake will sit on your stomach for a few minutes and then you're hungry again. Pumpkin pie, yes—the sugar just gives a little energy boost, but the pumpkin will keep you full for a while, plus it's full of vitamins and minerals."

Zetta met eyes with her aunt, certain she would burst out laughing at any moment. Pie, good for breakfast. But she seemed serious. And it was definitely tastier than her grandfather's obsession—baked potatoes for breakfast, lunch, and dinner—and more appetizing than that suspicious stew, so Zetta wasn't about to complain.

Aunt Meryl grabbed a pack and went outside. Zetta swallowed what she had in her mouth, then ran after her, watching as her aunt pulled carrots from the small gated garden behind the house. The rabbits all came running, and Aunt Meryl tossed the larger carrots to them.

"It's always better to grow your own ingredients when you can so you can be assured of the freshness. Carrots, for example, need to be picked while they're still tender. After a season, they get tough and start to lose their potency. You can pick them a few days ahead of when you need them. Just be sure to store them without their green tops so they don't lose all their moisture."

Zetta nodded, then pulled a carrot and held it up to the brown plump rabbit milling around, confused by her presence. She moved the carrot a little closer, and the rabbit inched a few steps toward her, its nose twitching nervously. Finally it took the carrot, looking pleased with itself.

"Do they have names?" Zetta said. She reached out to give the brown rabbit a good scritching behind the ears, but it startled and took off to the other side of the garden with its loot.

"No. Don't get too attached . . ." Aunt Meryl said. "We won't have time for leaping potions, but, well, yeah . . ."

"Oh," Zetta said, remembering that the primary ingredient for leaping potions was a rabbit's foot. "Yeah." Having spent so much time on her grandparents' farm, Zetta knew better than to grow too fond of the animals. Sooner or later, they'd be on someone's dinner plate.

"On the other hand, fermented spider eyes — those last forever. In fact, the older they are, the better. I've had some of them for longer than you've been alive." Meryl's hard demeanor cracked along the edges as she became lost in thought. Zetta remembered her aunt only barely, but knew they'd once spent lots of time together when her parents were both off at work.

Aunt Meryl gathered other various items from around the garden — melons and sugarcane and mushrooms — and stuck them in her pack, then headed back to the house. Before going up the stairs, she peeked under the porch at the nether wart growing quietly in the dark. Maybe not so quietly — Zetta could swear she heard whispers. The hairs on the back of her neck rose. It took every single nerve she had not to bolt while she watched her aunt reach out among the red, warty growths, probing each gently with the tip of her index finger before stuffing a few in her bag.

"Is there anything to do about the smell of the nether wart?" Zetta asked, hoping there was a little magic to be had there. Some sort of potion that could make her sense of smell disappear, maybe.

"Just keep flowers about. Dried. Fresh-cut. Potpourri. In pots. Sooner or later, you get used to it." Aunt Meryl frowned. "Mostly. The older stuff will definitely curl your nose hairs, so you want to keep your nether wart as fresh as possible. That means you need your own farm. I can give you a couple blocks of soul sand to take back with you, but you need to make sure to keep it somewhere secure, because soul sand in the wrong hands can cause some serious problems. Your nether wart farm needs to be somewhere you frequent, probably close to your house. You don't want it left unattended for too long, especially around animals. Or impressionable people. But also keep it at least ten blocks away from where you sleep at night."

Zetta nodded vigorously, but she wanted Aunt Meryl to finish talking so they could head back into the house and start on the brewing. The whispers were becoming more intense. She could feel them running down her skin now, like the touch of a cold, dead finger.

Aunt Meryl patted her plump packful of brewing ingredients, then took a step up onto the raised porch. Zetta scurried after her, but when she tried to enter the front door, her aunt's hand pressed out. "Not so fast. You need to gather your ingredients first."

"But we just—" Zetta stammered.

"No, I just collected the ingredients for my brewing. Now you need to go collect yours. Just remember everything I said and you should be fine."

Zetta gulped and startled at the cold grip of a hand around her wrist, tugging her. But when she looked down, there was nothing there.

"It's fine. Everything's fine," Zetta mumbled to herself. "It's just hundreds of tortured souls that have been trapped in sand for probably thousands of years. What could possibly go wrong?"

Zetta closed her eyes and reached under the porch. Her fingers brushed up against the warty protrusions, and she picked the biggest she could find in the few seconds she dared to linger. Then she pulled her hand back and stuffed the nether wart into her pack without looking. She scrambled away until she hit the fence around the garden patch, then sucked in a cool breath, instantly soothing her aching lungs. She hadn't even realized she'd stopped breathing.

But now the worst part was over and out of the way, and she could gather the remaining ingredients without all that fear in her head. She picked out a plump, ripe melon. Melons took up a lot of space in the garden, but Aunt Meryl had said that they produced well once established.

She grabbed a dozen tender carrots, young and firm, and ripped their greens off before putting them in her pack. Then she picked a couple more to give to the rabbits milling about. Zetta was determined to redeem herself with that brown bunny, but when she went to look for it, she saw it bolting out of the gate she'd forgotten to close behind her.

"Oh no," Zetta said. She ran after the bunny, making sure to shut the gate this time. She clicked her tongue at the rabbit to get its attention. "Here, sweetie," Zetta said, offering a carrot to the rabbit as it crouched by a spruce tree. The rabbit twitched its nose, maybe a little interested. Good. But then Zetta noticed the mushrooms growing in the podsol at her feet. Might as well collect them now. She reached down slowly, grabbing a handful, then turned her focus back to the rabbit, but it was darting again . . . straight under the porch.

Zetta's heart stopped. No.

No. No. No.

Aunt Meryl had said something about animals and soul sand, hadn't she? She couldn't just leave the rabbit under there and hope it came back out. And she couldn't go running to her aunt for help. If she couldn't be trusted to close a gate properly, how was her aunt going to trust her with magic potions? No. She just had to be brave and crawl under there and grab the rabbit. It wouldn't take long. Fifteen seconds, max. And the voices, well, she would ignore them . . .

CHAPTER
SIX

When Zetta got on her hands and knees and peeked under the porch, she saw a pair of beady eyes staring out at her from the dark. For a second, she thought she saw them glowing red, like that killer rabbit Ashton was always going on about. But killer rabbits weren't real, just another made-up mob to keep people afraid. Zetta gulped. She was afraid. A little. The rabbit's eyes were back to normal now. Probably just a weird trick of the light.

You could always scare the rabbit out, a whisper said, running gently down her spine. It was a kind voice. Not that scary, even if it was from some poor long-dead soul.

She shook the voice off and tried to will herself forward, but it wasn't working. She was petrified to go under the porch.

Try building a scarecrow, the voice suggested. *Works for birds. Why not bunnies?*

Why not indeed. She wouldn't have to get all dirty and the

bunny would run out on its own. Win-win situation, right? But what could she build a scarecrow out of? Her grandpa used hay bales and pumpkins to keep the pests out of his potato patch, but Zetta didn't see either of those hanging about.

Soul sand. Four blocks of it, the voice said. *So simple. Just put it in a T shape . . .*

Mmmm. Aunt Meryl had said that she would give Zetta some soul sand of her own, so she probably wouldn't mind if Zetta collected it now. She dug up four blocks of sand with the least mature warts on them, then assembled them on the other side of the porch where the bunny was holed up.

Didn't look scary to Zetta, though. It needed a head.

A head, or perhaps three, . . . said the voice. *Behind the house, there's a chest buried down deep. There are three skulls inside. They'll do quite nicely.*

It seemed like a lot of work, digging all that way down, when she could have crawled in and out from under the porch several times over by now, but Zetta didn't question it. And she didn't question *why* she didn't question it. She didn't have to. It all made perfect, logical sense.

It took her ten minutes, but she finally had the chest unearthed. It looked very old—rusty hinges and splitting wood. And sure enough, inside were three black skulls. Zetta smiled to herself. They were definitely scary. So scary, she knew deep in her heart that she normally wouldn't come within a mile of such things, but now, they seemed harmless. Like children's toys. A little damp and fleshy in some places, with bits of rotting sinew clinging to the bone, but children's toys nonetheless.

She carried the skulls back to her scarecrow and set one in the middle. The voice was right. If one head was scary, three would definitely do the trick. She stacked another to the right, then was reaching down for the last skull when her aunt came screaming out of the house.

"Zetta! No! Don't!" she said, hopping over the railing of the porch and landing on the ground with a dramatic thud.

Do it. Now! the voice demanded. Not so gently this time.

"Zetta, love, put the skull down," said Aunt Meryl. She seemed afraid of Zetta in the same way Zetta had been afraid of the bunny's haunting red eyes.

Place the skull, Zetta.

Zetta's fingers trembled as she held the skull within inches of the soul sand. She wasn't sure who to listen to—the aunt who'd once coddled and spoiled Zetta as a toddler or this mysterious and definitely not nefarious voice emanating from haunted sand.

Zetta didn't get to make the choice, though, because in that moment of hesitation, her aunt came barreling at her and knocked her to the ground. The skull went tumbling out of her hands and bumped up against a planterful of daisies. It was an odd sight, something so grotesque huddled up close to something so beautiful.

"Zetta? Zetta, are you with me?" her aunt said, slapping her cheek.

Zetta shook the cobwebs from her mind. What was she doing out here? Why had her aunt tackled her?

"Hi, Aunty," Zetta muttered. "I'm sorry, I'm just having a hard time with thinking right now. Did I do something wrong?"

Aunt Meryl shook her head. "No, it's my fault for thinking this was even a remotely good idea. You're not ready. For goodness' sake, you almost created a—" Aunt Meryl bit her tongue.

Zetta looked over at the scarecrow. It was coming back to her now. The rabbit had gotten under the porch, and then she'd heard . . . "The whispers. They made me do that, didn't they?"

"I'd forgotten how persuasive they can be to those who aren't used to dealing with them. Some people are good at tuning the voices out, or maybe their minds are too busy to really listen. But the souls, they're always looking for a ready and willing target." Aunt Meryl helped Zetta back to her feet. "We'll get you cleaned up. I'll pack you a few pies to take with you on your way home."

"Wait, I thought we were going to brew!" Zetta held up her pack brimming with ingredients. "I'm almost done. I just need to collect some sugarcane!"

"I can't, Zetta."

"But the illagers!"

"I'll load you up with as many potions as you can carry, but I'm not teaching you. Your father—"

"What about my father? Why do you keep ignoring my questions about him? What's going on between you two?"

Aunt Meryl chewed her lip, the sadness in her eyes undeniable. Then she turned and walked to the back edge of the property, where the trees became denser. Zetta was about to sulk off in the other direction, when her aunt called, "Well, are you coming or what?"

Zetta scurried behind her aunt, hanging vines slapping her in the face, stepping over fallen trees that had rotted through. Among the shadows, Zetta caught glimpses of red eyes watching them — spiders — but somehow she knew they wouldn't approach as long as she was with her aunt. They came to a sheer drop and a view of the entire Overworld beyond the mountain. It seemed to go on and on, so crisp, like it was a painting. She sat down next to her aunt, as if they were about to have this conversation on the sofa and not on the precipice of a drop that would kill her if she slipped and fell.

Aunt Meryl sighed, her eyes tight on the horizon. "Your mother, she was brilliant. I don't know if your father ever told you that, but she was. She'd see a problem and come up with a dozen ways to fix it. She'd fix problems we didn't even know were problems."

"Really?" Zetta asked. She knew so little of her mother. Her father hardly ever spoke of her.

"Really. You know the piston door to the vault in the town hall? She invented that."

Zetta's eyebrows arched. She'd had no idea.

"Your mother and I, we became like sisters. We were inseparable. Your father was off mining for much of the day, so we kept each other company, especially after you were born. We took turns watching you while we worked. Me and my magic, her and her inventions.

"I made swiftness potions for the miners, to help them speed through the mining tunnels a little faster and to help them get home quicker, so they could spend more time with their families. Your mother even made a sugarcane farm that was fully automated to keep up with the demand. Our plan worked for a while. Your father was ecstatic with the productivity. Magic was still new to our town then, but everyone seemed to embrace it.

"Your mother and I worked together for months, trying to research even better ways to increase mining efficiency. We scoured the library for ideas, until one day she stumbled upon a brief mention of a device that could create haste magic. With this, your father and the other workers could mine at a quicker rate. The beacon would send out a magical force to anyone in range."

"Sounds perfect," Zetta said, imagining how much free time she could have had to practice her brewing skills if her mining sessions hadn't lasted all day. But obviously something had gone wrong, because she'd been mining for half a year now and had never even heard of a haste beacon.

"There was a catch. You needed a nether star to get it," Aunt Meryl said.

Everything Zetta knew about the nether came from the paper flower floats at the Eve of Hostile Mobs parade. Lava lakes. Angry pigs. Fireball-shooting ghasts floating around in midair. Zetta had believed in such fantastical beasts when she was little, but she knew it was all a trick to keep kids from being curious about traveling outside the town's borders, and the possibility of traveling outside of the Overworld for that matter. "So you went to the nether?"

"Didn't have to. I had soul sand from my nether wart farm and traded some other valuables for the wither skulls. You stack the sand just the right way and place the skulls on top, and you get a wither. A monstrosity that can wreak more havoc than almost any mob there is. It flies in the air, and has three heads that shoot skulls, each with more explosive power than a creeper. But if you manage to kill a wither, it'll drop a single, perfect nether star."

Zetta stiffened. The sudden movement reminded her that she was perched precariously on a cliff. She shifted her weight back. "That thing I built back there . . . I was creating a wither?"

"Nearly did. Would have torn this whole mountainside up." Aunt Meryl shrugged. "But that didn't happen, so don't worry yourself over it. Your mother wasn't worried either. She had an idea to kill a wither, a machine that would fire arrows and splash it with potions all at once, and when it died, we could claim the nether star it dropped and use it for the beacon."

Zetta's voice softened. "And her invention . . . it didn't work?"

"It was flawless. The wither only managed to fire one skull shot, which hit a poor, defenseless chicken. The machine wailed upon that wither, spending its full arsenal in a matter of seconds. Before we knew it, that overpowered mob was knocked out of existence, leaving only the nether star behind. We had our star!

"It was so beautiful, Zetta, you wouldn't believe. Shone so bright, we could barely stand to look at it. Everything had gone so right. And then your mother saw another treasure . . . a beautiful black rose lying on the ground. She collected it, and when we got home, your mother planted it to commemorate our success. But she must have gotten nicked by a thorn. She let out a cry of pain and was thrown back."

Zetta wasn't breathing again. And she had a warm tear running down her cheek. Her aunt Meryl's hand slipped into hers.

"It was a wither rose, created when the wither killed the chicken. I know that now, but back then, I was clueless. It usually isn't fatal, but your mother must have had some severe reaction to it, and got sicker and sicker. We suspected milk would cure it, but back then Sienna Dunes didn't have a cow. I told your father what happened and he sat by her side as I prepared healing potion after healing potion for her. She couldn't keep them down. Splash potions didn't work either. After a few hours, she just sort of withered away.

"We were all devastated, of course. Your father never really recovered. He took the star, probably tossed it off a cliff. Said there would be no more magic in his house, and in the whole of the town if he had his way. The others agreed and closed their minds off to the world and its possibilities. They were more than happy to stay stuck in their old ways, but what they didn't understand was that the world would keep changing, even if they kept ignoring it. So I had to keep practicing alchemy. I had to keep learning. It was the only thing that kept my mind off your mother and my loss. Our loss. I left Sienna Dunes after another six months. I never returned."

"I'm sorry," Zetta said, squeezing her aunt's hand.

"No, I'm sorry," Aunt Meryl said. "I thought we'd taken every precaution. We thought it was safe, that we were doing the right thing. But magic can be unpredictable. As soon as you get comfortable with it, it'll let you know who's really in charge." Aunt Meryl sighed, then pulled her hands into her lap, fiddling with her thumb. "That's her tunic you're wearing, isn't it?"

Zetta looked down at the frayed edge of the old blue tunic, then nodded. "I found it in a chest in the hall closet a few years back. It finally fits me. I think it's the first thing I've worn that's not green or lime green or white."

"You favor her. And she would have loved to see you like this, pursuing your own dreams and passions."

"I hope one day I can make her proud," Zetta said, twiddling her own thumbs now.

"You will. And I suppose it wouldn't be the worst thing if I help hasten that along . . ."

"Does that mean—" Zetta began, forgetting herself again, and shifting so quickly that she nearly slipped off the edge of the cliff. Her aunt's hand reached out and grabbed her.

Aunt Meryl nodded. "I'll give you exactly *one* brewing lesson. So get your questions ready—you've got to make them count."

Zetta followed her aunt back home, her head dizzy with excitement, and soon her aunt was giving Zetta her first official brewing lesson.

"You have to keep the swiftness potions on low heat so the sugar doesn't caramelize," Aunt Meryl was saying, wiping the sweat from her forehead. They had taken out another set of four brewing stands and placed them on the opposite side of the workbench for Zetta to use. With eight brewing stands going at the same time, and even with the windows open, the whole room was beyond steamy.

Zetta jotted a note in her book, then went over to one of the bubbling potions and reduced the heat to low. The bubbles died down. She added a heaping scoop of sugar, pleased when the potion faded into a blue the exact same shade as the one her aunt was brewing. Zetta didn't have time to let out a breath, though. Her aunt was going a million miles an hour, like she'd downed a swiftness potion already, but it was just nerves and excitement, Zetta knew. Aunt Meryl probably didn't get to talk to people much, and even as much of a recluse as she was, Zetta could tell that she was enjoying the company and a chance to pass down her knowledge.

"The amount of blaze powder you add to a strength potion depends on the ambient temperature of the room. If it's warm, you can use a little less. Daytime brewing will work well for you in the desert, so take advantage of that. You might not notice the difference when making single potions, but if you're working with a big batch, those savings add up." Zetta watched carefully as Aunt Meryl threw a handful of blaze powder into another awkward potion.

She didn't have any of the potions labeled, which made Zetta uncomfortable. Zetta didn't want to lose track of which awkward potion was getting which additional ingredients, so she drew a diagram in her notebook and carefully wrote down what had been added to each. Her aunt seemed pleased with this thoroughness, though she expressed this in the form of arched brows and pinched lips instead of praise.

Then Aunt Meryl went to her crafting table and slammed a

whole melon on it. She cut into it, revealing bright red flesh. After a couple of abrupt slices, she took out some gold nuggets and worked them into a glistering, perfect fruit.

As soon as she was done, she diced it quickly, then practically sprinted over to the brewing stand and dumped the chunks into the glass bottles. "Glistering melons can be tricky to work with and get juice all over the place. So if you don't want an impossibly sticky mess to clean out of your inventory, you should craft them right before use. Seeds are fine. You can strain them out after the brewing is complete, if you like."

Zetta nodded, then crafted her melon, and somehow, despite the warning, still got juice all over her clothes. Plus, her chunks were too big to fit in the mouths of the bottles, so she had to go back and cut all the pieces in half. Then, frazzled, she wiped the sweat from her forehead, leaving sticky residue on her face as well.

The golden carrots were a lot easier—no cutting them into smaller bits. Finally, she had the healing, strength, swiftness, and regeneration potions all going at the same time. Zetta double-, triple-, and quadruple-checked her notes as she worked. She couldn't afford to mess this opportunity up.

"Now, the moment of truth . . ." Aunt Meryl said. "You know about adding gunpowder to make splash potions. Accuracy is important there. You can use this scoop, level off the top. No more, no less, or things can quickly get out of hand. Other options are to strengthen your potion with glowstone or lengthen its duration with redstone. A handful of each is all you need. Go ahead and experiment. Spotting the optimal consistency comes with time, and you'll get a sense of exactly when to take the potions off the burners."

Zetta tossed a handful of glowstone into the swiftness potion and a handful of redstone into the strength potion. The transparent liquid went cloudy in both as the dust dissolved. Flecks of glowstone caught the light, mesmerizing Zetta. But she pulled away and carefully measured out some gunpowder. She took the scoop and collected a heap, then slid her finger across the top of the scoop, knocking the excess back into the barrel. She held her breath as she dumped it into the healing potion, but as soon as she was done, she got drawn in by the glowstone flecks in the swiftness potion again. So pretty.

Maybe she was staring too hard, because she was caught off guard by the most amazing scent, like dessert. She was about to ask her aunt if she had some sweets cooking for lunch, when she realized the swiftness potion had started to caramelize, leaving the bottom of the glass bottle coated in a warm, golden goo.

"Drat!" Zetta said. It didn't look salvageable. "I thought I had it on the lowest setting," she said.

Aunt Meryl came over, inspected the brewing stand's blaze powder container, its energy source, and shook her head. "This stand always used to give me trouble. It wasn't you—just some clogged feed tubes. I'll get this cleaned up and you can try again."

Zetta sighed, relieved that it wasn't her fault. She didn't know what she'd do if she'd botched a potion like that. Still, she had the other potions left, and she had to get those right. What had she been doing?

Oh, the splash potion. Her nerves were rattled, but she shook it off and carefully measured out some gunpowder. She took the scoop and collected a heap, then slid her finger across the top of the scoop, knocking the excess back into the barrel. She held her breath as she dumped it into the healing potion, and . . .

The brewing stand sparked and fizzled violently. Wait, how much gunpowder had she added? Zetta had seen this before: the time she'd lost her eyebrows in her first brewing experiment. The blaze powder had ignited that time and had caused a small explosion. Now that Zetta knew more about how brewing stands worked, she could stop it. She twisted the container off and quickly emptied the blaze powder onto the workbench. The brewing stand quieted, and the powder's sizzle began to dissipate.

The little pile of dust sent off one last spark, like a single orange firework arching through the room. Zetta's eyes went wide as she traced its trajectory to the chest, brimming with blaze powder, the lid still open. Zetta tried to get there in time to close it, but it was too late. The spark landed in the chest, and—

Bam!

Zetta's vision went white and her ears rang louder than Sienna Dunes' bell tower. It took her a moment to realize that she was no longer standing upright, but instead was wedged between a crafting table and a chest. She blinked several times, and slowly the ringing faded and her vision fully returned. The entire brewing station and much of Aunt Meryl's alchemy room had been obliterated.

CHAPTER
SEVEN

Aunt Meryl rushed back into the room in a panic, and without another thought, ran to a nearby cauldron and used a bucket to scoop out water to extinguish the various small fires that had spread around the room. She doused what was left of the blaze powder chest until every last ember was soaked and no longer a threat. Aunt Meryl's alchemy room was now a sad combination of charred and soggy.

She stooped down beside Zetta. Her mouth was going a million miles a minute, but Zetta could only catch bits and pieces of what she was saying over the thudding headache. Zetta knew her aunt was very cross with her; that much was clear. What an awful mistake.

Zetta started groveling. She didn't know what else to do. "I'm so sorry, Aunty! Please don't tell my father. I'll do whatever you want! Clean your house. Cook your stew. Tend your gardens.

Fetch you stuff from town. Anything that doesn't involve potions. I'll work off the mess I've caused. I promise I will."

Aunt Meryl sighed. "You've made a mess, for sure, but the important thing is that you're all right. I can always craft more brewing stands. What I can't craft is another one of you." Aunt Meryl sighed again, looking around at all the damage. "You know, your mother and I had our share of disasters when we were first starting out. Once, I was trying to make a fire resistance potion and must have put in too much magma cream. I chugged down the bottle, then stepped into a fire to see what would happen." Aunt Meryl leaned in and her eyes got wide.

"What happened?" Zetta asked.

"You know that weird scorch mark on the back of Nana and Papa's barn?"

Zetta nodded.

"I lit up so bright and threw off so much heat that I singed everything within five blocks of me. Nearly burnt down the barn. Needless to say, I've gotten pretty quick at putting out fires." She smiled warmly at Zetta. "And if I had a gold ingot for every time one of your mother's contraptions nearly knocked my head off, I could build myself a four-level beacon. She started keeping meticulous notes in leather-bound journals, and after that, she stopped making so many mistakes. Accidents happen, Zetta. It's part of the process of learning. Just next time, try not to make such an expensive one." Meryl winced as she looked around again. The sighs just kept coming.

"The potions are all ruined, and it looks like I'm out of blaze powder. I can't send you back empty-handed. I'll go fetch some more. You can work on cleaning up this mess while I'm gone."

Zetta nodded. "Anything. Thank you, Aunty."

"And look after the animals and gardens. And please, please, don't go anywhere near a brewing stand or the soul sand. And try not to break anything else," Aunt Meryl said, lifting a lid on a chest on the other side of the room. She pulled out a sword. Not iron. Not diamond. It was black and sleek and looked sharp enough to slice through a sheet of paper, edgewise. Then Aunt Meryl pulled out a blue-gray cape and tied it on tight. It hung down her back, almost like the wings of a bee.

Finally, her aunt pulled a glimmering bow from her chest and arrows that looked different from the white ones Rayne used. They had colored tips, and tiny particles danced around them like dust motes. "Ummm . . ." Zetta said, clearing her throat. "What's going on there? Those arrows look . . . magic."

"That's because they are. Dipped in splash potions laced with dragon's breath. Poison. Harming. Weakness." She frowned. "Sadly, not a lesson we'll get to. I'm afraid I'm done with apprentices for now."

Zetta couldn't argue. She'd been studying under her aunt for not even half a day, and she'd already nearly summoned a wither and destroyed much of her aunt's livelihood. Her aunt had every right to be disappointed. Zetta watched as her aunt kept pulling more and more items from the chest and storing them away in her inventory. It seemed a bit excessive for a quick trip.

"Wait, how long will you be gone exactly?" Zetta asked, setting one of the busted brewing stands upright. Blaze powder had fused to the inside casing, beyond useless now. Zetta knew the closest town was quite a hike, but it wouldn't require more than an overnight stay . . . maybe two, if Aunt Meryl wanted to enjoy the sights.

"One week, two weeks max," Aunt Meryl said. "I have to make a run to the nether. I'll pick up some other ingredients while I'm there. I'm running a little low on ghast tears anyway." She said this so casually, it was like she was about to go out back to pull some carrots. Like going to the nether was just an everyday activity, not crossing over into a lava-plagued underworld.

"Wait . . . ghasts are actually real?"

"Where did you think ghast tears came from?" Aunt Meryl asked.

"I don't know, I just thought it was named that to make it sound cooler. Like magma cream or phantom membranes or . . . or dragon's breath."

Aunt Meryl sighed again. "Oh, my dear child. We'll have to have a long talk when I get back. I'll promise to be as quick as I can, but I've got a lot to replace. It sounds like you gave those illagers a good wallop, though, so it'll take them a while to recover and regroup for another attack."

"Okay, well, I'll clean up and dust all the cobwebs while you're away," Zetta mumbled. "And I'll have a bunch of pumpkin pies ready for your return."

"Leave the cobwebs," Aunt Meryl said, patting Zetta's cheek.

"They give the place some character. And I look forward to the pies. Hopefully you're a better baker than an alchemist." She said this jokingly, to lighten the mood, but it only made Zetta feel worse. Zetta wanted to shrink up inside herself, but she managed to put on a smile.

"Let's hope," she said.

After her aunt departed, Zetta started the long process of picking up glass shards and mopping up her spilled hopes and dreams. Miraculously, one of her potions had survived the explosion. A strength potion. The bottle was still warm to the touch and held a bloodred liquid. She packed it into her inventory, tucking away just a little bit of optimism with it. But maybe her father was right. Maybe she needed to stop worrying about potions and let the adults worry about keeping Sienna Dunes safe.

It took her two whole days, but finally, the place was gleaming. Zetta poked around the room some, peeking in chests. One of the chests contained a bunch of sand. Zetta thought it might be nice to craft some glass bottles to replace all the ones she'd ruined, so she stoked the furnace.

While she was waiting for it to heat up so she could make glass, she looked at the curiosities stored on high shelves. She wouldn't touch, of course. No way would she risk ruining her aunt's trust further. Green-eyed totems lined one shelf, seven of them all in a row. Were those emeralds?

Odd-looking purple fruits sat on another shelf. Zetta got close enough to smell them. Sweet, but in an otherworldly sort of way that left an odd, tacky taste in the back of her throat. Another chest contained ender pearls. Zetta and her friends were never brave enough to fight endermen, but sometimes other hunting parties brought pearls back. These looked different, though. A lighter shade of green, and the pupils seemed like they were watching her. She shut the chest quickly as a chill ran down her spine.

Then Zetta caught a glimpse of something in the far corner of the room—the darkest corner of the room, where the light from the windows and torches didn't quite reach. It was buried under tons of cobwebs, like it had been sitting there for a decade.

It was an egg. Zetta could just barely make it out. A large egg, nearly half as tall as she was. The deepest, most beautiful black, with specks of purple all over. It called to her, like a song.

Zetta was wary. She didn't want another wither incident for sure, but dusting it off a little wouldn't be such a bad thing, right? Sure, cobwebs made the place look lived in, but this . . . this was a little much. And the egg was so pretty. It should be shown off, right? Put on display?

So Zetta dusted a little around the edges, until more and more of the egg was showing. There. Much better. She stood next to it, hands on her hips, triumphant. Now, to get started on making that glass.

But her feet didn't move her toward the fiery furnace. Not even one step.

"Now, to get starting on making that glass!" she said, aloud this time, hoping her body would take the hint. But she was stuck looking at this egg, this thing of beauty.

She shouldn't touch it.

She shouldn't.

But the softest, most delicate poke with her finger wouldn't hurt, would it? It's not like she would break it. This thing was old, but it didn't look fragile. Looked as tough as a rock, actually.

"Those bottles aren't going to make themselves," Zetta said one last time, pleading with her conscience as her index finger extended toward the egg.

She touched it, and immediately felt a strange suction and heard a loud pop echo through the room. She blinked. Once. Twice. Zetta gritted her teeth.

Good news was that she didn't break the egg.

Bad news was that it had disappeared. Completely.

"Okay, not completely," Zetta said with a sigh of relief, realizing the egg was now behind her. She'd nearly tripped over it. She reached down so she could put it back in the dark corner, but as soon as she touched it, it blinked away again, this time reappearing on the brewing counter. She tried again, moving as slowly as she could, but it blinked away and plopped down in front of the door, like it was trying to escape.

Panic grew in the pit of Zetta's stomach, making her as queasy as she had been staring into her aunt's suspicious stew. She had to fix this. Fast. Moving the egg by hand clearly was not going to work. She felt like maybe if she used her brain, she could figure out a solution. Zetta hoped that her mother's ingenuity had been passed down to her. Zetta knew her mother had made mistakes, too, but she was desperate not to make another one.

She had to figure out a way to get that egg back in its place. She tried poking it with a stick. It didn't disappear, at least, but when she tried pushing it with the stick, the egg proved too heavy and didn't budge. What Zetta needed was something to give her a little leverage. Instantly, her mind went to pistons. She'd seen Rift use them in his redstone contraption pranks. If she could craft one, maybe she could use it to scoot the egg back into place.

It took her a little trial and error on the crafting table to figure out how to make the piston and a little lever to go with it, but Zetta did it. She set the piston on the ground and the lever next to it. She pulled it a few times, and squealed with delight as the piston's head popped in and out, in and out.

But when she faced the piston at the egg and pulled the lever, it stuck. Or the egg weighed too much. She pulled harder, and the piston started to inch the egg forward ever so slightly, but it was just too tough. Zetta wasn't strong enough.

Zetta pulled out her strength potion. She'd promised her aunt that she wouldn't craft any potions, but she hadn't said anything about using potions that were already made. She uncorked her potion. Before the explosion, Zetta had been sure the potions she'd brewed were all perfectly fine. She'd be fine. Zetta gulped.

She put the bottle to her lips, the hot, almost burning liquid slipping down the back of her throat. Zetta sucked in cool breaths rapidly. The potion didn't have a distinct flavor, other than the lingering aftertaste of nether wart, but her tongue felt like she'd licked the surface of the sun.

Nearly instantly, she felt a tightening in her body like, though she was still contained in her original skin, she'd grown to twice her size. It felt like there was suddenly so much more of her. And beyond feeling stronger, there was now an itch in her mind to *use* that power. To show it off.

Zetta stared down the egg. It didn't have eyes, but it was definitely staring back. She decided to show it who was boss, and pulled the lever with all her might.

Maybe it was too much might, because the head of the piston shot out with a tremendous force, and instead of the egg moving, the piston. . . .

. . . cracked it.

Zetta's eyes went wide as the crack lengthened and deepened. Oh no.

No. No. No.

What had she done? Glass bottles and potion ingredients could be replaced, but this? Aunt Meryl would never forgive Zetta for breaking this egg. The crack ran clear from the top to the bottom, and was so wide she could stick her hand in it if she wanted to. No way could it be repaired.

And what was worse, *really* worse, was that she could see something moving inside.

CHAPTER
EIGHT

Zetta screamed.

Whatever was inside the egg squealed in response—an odd noise caught between a kitten's purr and a bat's shriek. Needle-sharp claws pried at the crack in the thick black shell, slowly crumbling it, until a nose poked through. The thing had big nostrils, like a cow, but was scaly, like a turtle. And the creature was the deepest, richest black—darker even than the shadowy egg it was emerging from.

"Stay in there," Zetta warned, taking three enormous steps back. "Don't come out! I'm a master potioner and you definitely don't want to mess with me." Without breaking focus on the hatching creature, she reached into her pack for a weapon, feeling around for something sharp and threatening, but she pulled out a stone hoe. Ack, not as good as a sword, but at least it could inflict some damage. Especially if this black nose turned out to be connected to an oversized carrot.

More of the shell crumbled, until the whole head and most of the body were free. Zetta stood there petrified. She didn't know what to make of it. Four legs, a long, scaly tail, and flappy wings that looked way too large for its body. Plus it had purple eyes similar to those of endermen, but sort of innocent and cute?

It was cute, like a little pup in most ways. It purred at her, then chirped, then gurgled. Its nostrils flared. The way it looked at her, it was all wrong.

"No, no, no . . ." Zetta said, holding the hoe up between them. "You've got the wrong idea. I am *not* your mama."

The creature took a few more timid steps toward Zetta, then chirped again, trilling up at the end, almost like it was asking a question. The creature nuzzled Zetta's waist. It was large, the size of a half-grown cow, but a lot stronger. It nearly knocked her over.

"I said, 'No.' Aunty Meryl will be home in a couple weeks. She'll know what to do with you, so just wait until then to start loving on somebody."

She tentatively patted it on the head, then backed up a few more steps, carefully moving the hoe between them again. But the creature bit the tool gently and began shaking it back and forth, like a dog with a stick. Zetta tried to tug it away from the beast, but it only got more excited, and its grip grew tighter, until the hoe's handle snapped clean in half.

Zetta shook her head, trying to ward off the truth. She was responsible for this mess, for looking after this creature, at least until her aunt got back. This was not the distraction she needed right now. Her town was in trouble, and she needed to figure out a way to help it that didn't involve exploding potions.

Zetta looked at the creature again, staring at those black scales and strong wings. Strange thoughts started to meander through her mind. This . . . whatever it was . . . seemed familiar to her somehow. She'd helped her cousin make a dragon costume that was black and scaly, just like this little beast. Ashton really bought into all that Eve of Hostile Mobs nonsense and had probably imagined up a new dangerous mob of his own. What had he called it? An ender dragon? Zetta always smiled and nodded when he showed her those silly little sketches he drew in his notebook. Ashton was just a kid, so what did he know? Heck, he still slept with a torchlight.

Besides, there was no way this cute creature could turn into something as menacing as a dragon. No purple poison spewed from its nostrils. It didn't have claws that could slice Zetta in half. Nor did it have the heft to deliver "dragon kisses," a strong hit with the end of its snout that would knock you into next week.

Ashton had a wonderfully overactive imagination, that was it. This was definitely not a dragon, just some sort of oversized bat. She could take care of it. Who knows, maybe if she did a good job, her aunt would see how responsible she actually was and reconsider training her on potions. It was a long shot, but Zetta didn't exactly have any other hopes to rest on right now, so she would put all her focus into raising this beast that was *definitely* not a dragon.

"Okay," Zetta said to the creature. "First things first. You're probably hungry after being inside an egg for the past decade, so what do you eat?"

The creature cocked its head.

Zetta fished around in her pack and laid out some carrots and a bowl of cold rabbit stew in front of the creature. It sniffed at both, then turned its head away with a huff.

"Not hungry—okay, got it. What do you want then?"

The creature came even closer, then jumped at Zetta. Her quick reactions allowed her to reach out her arms and catch the baby beast. It nuzzled her neck as she struggled to keep it snuggled upon her chest. She gave it a little hug and the beast purred in her ear. She could feel it through her body as well, a slight vibration that put a smile on her face. Maybe she'd enjoy this time with her new not-so-little little friend.

All of a sudden, her muscles started straining. Her insides felt like they were folding back up, her inner strength collapsing like a stack of scaffolding. The strength potion. It was wearing off. Zetta's muscles shook, trying to keep the creature tucked safely in her arms, but they gave out, and she dropped the poor creature on the hard floor. It let out an alarmed cry, then gave her pouty eyes. It looked at her with all the disappointment in the world.

Zetta tried to apologize, but the baby beast was inconsolable and started snorting and galloping all over the workshop, knocking over bottles and overturning chests, and threatening to make an even worse mess than Zetta had caused with the explosion. She was starting to realize that this wasn't a cute little creature, but instead a force of destruction.

Aunt Meryl had warned Zetta not to have any more big mess-ups, but there was nothing bigger than this. Getting this creature out of here was Zetta's first priority. She opened the door, whistled at it, cooed, then tried speaking to it in a high-pitched voice.

"Who's a good beastie?" she said, imitating how her cousin Ashton talked to the farm animals. "Who's the best beastie in the whole wide Overworld?"

The creature looked at Zetta with mistrust in its eyes, then snuffed.

It liked sticks. She pulled a stick from her pack and waggled it in front of the creature. It didn't look impressed.

"Okay, something bigger, right?" She borrowed a bit of wood from her aunt's stash, then crafted a wooden shovel, dull enough that it wouldn't hurt anyone. When she was done, she took a piece of charcoal and drew eyes and a friendly smile on the face of the shovel. "Do you like this?" she asked, holding the shovel out to the creature that was definitely not a dragon. "Come on, I know you want it."

The creature took a step forward. And another. Zetta took a step back toward the door.

"We can play fetch outside. Outside and away from all of these fragile objects."

The creature wagged its tail, knocking over a cauldron with dank purple liquid inside. Zetta winced, but the creature didn't even notice. It took several bouncy steps toward her. She turned and rushed out the front door, the dragon, err . . . not-a-dragon following behind her. When she was on the porch, she threw the shovel as far as she could.

The creature flapped its wings as it ran, but couldn't get off the ground. It pounced on the shovel, then picked it up in its slobbery maw and shook it violently from side to side.

"Careful," Zetta said. "Don't break that one. Gentle. Gentle."

The creature trotted back to Zetta and dropped the slobber-covered shovel at her feet.

"You like that, huh?" She picked the shovel up again and tossed it even farther. The creature darted after it again. And again. At first, Zetta was having fun, letting loose, but after the twelfth throw, her arm began aching and the game was getting old. The creature, however, was far from done playing.

"Don't you eat? Or sleep? Or just . . ." Ugh. She was going to need some help with this. Rift and Rayne would have some idea of what to do, but she couldn't exactly stroll back into town with a beast like this. And she couldn't leave it at her aunt's place. It would smash the whole house apart by sunset.

So Zetta decided to split the difference . . . take the dragon somewhere safe, and then fetch her friends. She packed herself a few of her aunt's pies for the trip, promising she'd come back to bake some replacements. Then she lured the dragon back down the mountain, shovel toss by shovel toss, until she came upon a cave that looked like as good a spot as any.

She peeked into the darkness, turning her ear and listening for the skittering of spiders or the clattering of skeleton bones, but she didn't hear anything. She ventured farther in, holding the shovel up for protection. The baby beast followed her in, its purple eyes glowing eerily in the dark.

The cave was deep and came to a dead end, perfect for stashing the not-a-dragon for a bit. She put out a cauldron of water and a few snacks for the creature, just in case it got hungry or thirsty, then backed up some. The poor thing would be cross with Zetta for this, but she didn't have a choice. She threw the shovel deep into the cave a few times, and the creature always came back with it, so happy, Zetta could swear it was smiling at her.

Each time it went to fetch the shovel, Zetta laid down a few more cobblestone bricks near the cave's entrance. Then Zetta did a fake throw of the shovel, and the baby beast fell for it and went loping deep into the cave, looking and searching frantically for the tool. It was gone for nearly a minute before it came back, sulking. By then, Zetta had closed off the entire opening of the cave, except for a small hole so the beast could get fresh air.

She peeked inside. Those cute puppy dog eyes eased into slits like those she would imagine on a giant, poison-breathing ender dragon, if she'd believed in that sort of thing. Which she didn't.

"Sorry, friend," Zetta said. "This is for your own good. I won't be gone long. I'll bring friends, okay? Rift is a bit of a jokester, but he's really smart. And Rayne is great with a bow and arrow and is the bravest person I know. You'll like them both."

The creature snorted.

Then the wall shook. Ugh. Zetta constructed a second layer of cobblestone, just to be safe. And a third. Then she took off back toward town.

CHAPTER
NINE

Rift looked at Zetta like she had a squid sitting on top of her head. "You say you've got a what now?"

"I don't know how to explain it. There was an egg, then it disappeared. Then it was back. Then I cracked it. Then this thing . . . hatched out of it."

"A cow? With scales?" Rayne said, nodding slowly.

"No, not a cow! It's almost as big as a cow. And it's scaly, yes, and black. And has wings, but I don't think it can fly yet." Zetta took a deep breath. They were at their secret meeting spot at her grandparents' farm. She couldn't risk going back home, so she'd stayed up here, in the rafters of the barn, trying to ignore the smell of chickens and pigs wallowing below.

"Just come. You have to see it to believe it. I have to take care of this thing until my aunt gets back, and I can't do it alone." Zetta shrugged.

"The town is still a mess, Zetta," Rayne said. "We just can't leave it." *Not like you did,* were the words that went unspoken. The twins had told Zetta about how her father had stopped by their home multiple times looking for her. She hadn't even told her friends where she was going, and she felt guilty for causing them to worry. Now she'd come back with this nonsense story and needed their help.

"Yeah, we need to prepare for the next attack," Rift continued. "Because there will be another."

"That's why I left! To figure out how to use potions better to help us defend Sienna Dunes. But then I almost conjured up a wither, destroyed my aunt's alchemy room twice, and broke an egg and released some kind of baby beast. I can't fix this by myself, but if I had your help . . ."

"Our parents aren't going to just let us leave for days on end," said Rayne. "We've got responsibilities here."

"I realize that," Zetta said. "That's why we'll split shifts, cover for one another. If we time things right, your parents won't even notice you're—"

A loud thump came from down below. Suddenly they were all on edge, nervous that someone had discovered their hiding spot. The three friends poked their heads over the lip of the barn rafters, staring down at the dirt floor below. Hay bales were stacked in the corners, and an old stone hoe was propped up against the back wall. A cranky chicken perched on top of a seed storage chest, like it was waiting for someone to open it.

"Hello?" Zetta called out. The only noise that came back was the grunt of a pig.

Rayne shrugged. "Don't see anyone. Pig probably knocked over a feeding trough or something."

Zetta let out a sigh. They couldn't afford to get caught now. Nana and Papa's farm had eyes, and not just the ones on Papa's potatoes. It was best not to linger. The friends climbed down a rickety ladder, then ran off to the town square. Most of the smaller messes had been cleared away, but the larger damage still lingered.

The bell tower was missing a huge chunk of sandstone near the bottom, looking as if it should topple over, but it still stood tall. Townspeople were working on adding a second layer to the wall, and Zetta pulled the loose fabric at the neck of her tunic up and over her nose, hoping no one would notice she was back. She was so caught up in not accidentally running into her father or the mayor that she nearly ran into the egg display outside the grocery store.

"Careful!" Gloriana the grocer said, holding her hands out so Zetta wouldn't knock over what looked to be at least a hundred eggs.

"Sorry," Zetta said, her voice slightly muffled by the fabric. She'd cracked quite enough eggs today already. She avoided eye contact with Gloriana as the friends ducked into the store to buy snacks for their adventure . . . can't sprint on an empty stomach. Between them, the friends had only five emeralds, but it was enough to purchase six loaves of bread and some sweet berries.

The friends then took off into the desert, running as fast as their legs would carry them, trying to avoid mobs when they could, and fighting them when they couldn't.

The desert scenery slowly became lusher. The sun became less oppressive, and the air became more humid. Patches of green oases started appearing here and there, until the friends found themselves in a new biome altogether.

Zetta saw the mountain off in the distance. She was tired and frustrated that they still had so far to go. The trip had already eaten up so much of the day. But they kept sprinting, nibbling on bread and berries every time they started slowing down.

Finally, they came to the cave entrance. "Okay, don't be scared," Zetta warned. "No sudden movements." She took the shovel out of her pack, hoping it would be a peace offering for the baby beast. But as they walked deeper into the cave, pieces of busted cobblestone crunched under Zetta's feet. Oh no, she thought. When she rounded the corner, she saw that the wall she'd built was totally smashed.

"So where's this creature?" Rayne asked. "Is it invisible, too?"

"I swear it was here! It busted through the wall."

Rift nodded. "Sure . . . Are you trying to prank us? Because you know that I'm going to prank you back even harder."

"No! The dragon is real. I saw it with my own—" Zetta clapped her hands over her mouth. She'd said the "d" word, hadn't she? She shook her head. "It's not a dragon. They don't exist. I'm not sure what the creature is. All I know is that it's still a baby and now it's lost somewhere out there, and we have to find it."

But before Zetta could turn around, she heard crunching cobblestone behind her. She'd been in such a hurry that she hadn't bothered to check the cave for mobs when they got here. It didn't sound clattery like a skeleton or skittery like a spider. Then she heard the moan.

Zombie. Definitely zombie. Hopefully just one. In an instant, all three friends had their weapons drawn. They crept toward the moaning noise. When they turned the corner, Zetta felt her blood go cold . . . not from fear, but from shock. Her little cousin Ashton was leaning against the cave wall, rubbing his arm.

"Ashton! How'd you get here?" Zetta asked.

"Ran, same as you," he said, still moaning.

"What's wrong with your arm?" Rift asked.

"I stopped to cool off for a bit in a lake," Ashton said sheepishly. "And some kind of super-soggy husk bit me. But I took it out with a couple swings of my sword."

Zetta rushed over to examine the bite. It wasn't deep. It'd heal quickly. Still, she was furious at her cousin for putting himself in danger. "You shouldn't have followed us. You're too young and inexperienced to be out here with hostile mobs about."

Ashton frowned, then reached into his pack and tossed a bunch of rotten flesh and some bones in front of Zetta. "I killed seven husks and four skeletons on my way here. It's not that hard. I don't know why you think I'm still a little kid. I'm practically as tall as you!"

Rift's eyes grew wide. "Your cousin is hard-core, Zetta. I don't know why you don't want him to hang out with us."

Zetta shot Rift a significant look. She didn't want Ashton to know that she was the reason he'd been excluded from their group.

Rift fumbled over his blunder and backtracked. "Uh, I mean, uhh . . . I don't know what I mean. Please don't listen to me. I wasn't even talking."

But it was too late. Ashton looked up at Zetta with the saddest puppy dog eyes.

"I want you to hang out with us," Zetta said, coming to her own defense, since Rift was being useless. "But skeletons and zombies are one thing, Ashton. This creature . . . I don't know what it is, and it's small now, but I can't risk having it turn and become something dangerous with you around."

"It's an ender dragon," Ashton said.

"You haven't even seen it," Zetta replied, rolling her eyes.

"I heard you describe it back in the barn." He pulled out his notebook and showed it to Zetta. She'd seen the sketch before — a big black dragon with a menacing glare. There was some resemblance, for sure . . . if the baby beast were about fifty times bigger and a million times meaner. "Reed told me about it once when I was browsing for books about hostile mobs. He told me a bunch of other stuff about it too that could help me track down the dragon, but since I'm still a kid and all, you probably just want me to go back home where it's nice and safe."

Zetta was taken aback by the resentment in Ashton's voice. Her cousin was usually so laid-back and positive about everything. She must have really wounded his pride. It was time for her to grovel.

"Ashton. You're right. I was wrong. It's just when I see you, I still have an image of that little kid I used to babysit in my mind.

Remember when we used to build sandcastles together and used to try to fish in the little pond behind the silo? But you're ready now. We want you on this adventure. Don't we?" Zetta asked, looking back at Rift and Rayne.

"Definitely!" they said in unison.

"So it's settled then?" Zetta asked, extending a hand to her cousin. "You'll help us find this . . ." The word didn't want to come out of her mouth again, but she forced it. ". . . this ender *dragon*."

Ashton stood up, tall and proud, and shook Zetta's hand. "This is going to be so awesome," he said. "Come on, follow me!" And then he was sprinting out of the cave like he'd never been injured at all. His eyes darted back and forth, searching the woods, looking for breaks in the foliage and branches that indicated something had passed through.

They waded across a stream full of salmon and trekked through a grove of giant dark oak trees. The canopy was so thick, the sun barely penetrated through the leaves. The forest floor was damp and cold, and the day was dragging into night, but every time Zetta thought Ashton had lost the dragon's trail, he'd spot a tree trunk missing a chunk or a big bush with a baby dragon–shaped hole punched through the leaves. Finally, they heard shuffling and grunting and a familiar purr.

Zetta held her shovel up, ready to entice the baby beast. "Who's a good little beastie?" she called out. "I've got your stick!"

Footsteps came toward her at a steady gallop. Heavy footsteps—and when the dragon broke through the undergrowth, everyone scattered and headed for cover. Rayne climbed up into a tree. Rift hid behind a boulder. Zetta dropped the shovel and took shelter behind a tree trunk.

"I thought you said this thing was the size of a cow," Rift said, head popping up from behind the boulder for a quick look.

Zetta took another peek as well. The beast was as big as one of those ravagers now, bulkier and with a longer tail and massive claws. It still had those big puppy dog eyes, though, and it sniffed the air, content to be playing whatever game it thought the friends were playing. Zetta gulped.

She wasn't sure how the dragon had grown so much, but this definitely wasn't a game.

CHAPTER
TEN

The dragon sniffed out Rayne first, then stood up on its hind legs and pushed at the tree with its front paws, mouthing a low-hanging limb. After a couple of playful shoves, its claws were tearing into the trunk, sending wood blocks flying in all directions. Its giant flapping wings weren't enough to get it off the ground, but they did stir fallen leaves and sticks and dirt into miniature vortices.

Zetta tried to call the dragon away, but terror had twisted her tongue in a knot. She didn't have a whole lot of experience with trees, but surely it would collapse, its leaves tumbling down around Rayne like falling sand. But the tree stood tall, despite missing half its trunk.

Ashton picked up the shovel Zetta had dropped and approached the beast. Zetta's fear for Rayne hadn't even subsided yet, and now here she was, getting a second dose, seeing her little cousin exposed to this unpredictably destructive creature.

"Ashton Alexander Night," Zetta said under her breath, thoroughly feeling like her father, "I swear you better step away right now before—"

Ashton extended his upturned palm to the dragon. "Who's the best ender dragon in the whole Overworld?" Ashton cooed at it. The dragon turned toward him with a big goofy grin on its face. It licked Ashton's palm, then his face, leaving a gloopy trail of slobber behind. Ashton didn't even flinch. He waved the shovel in front of the dragon, and its tail started wagging, smashing the earth beneath it.

"That's a good dragon," Ashton said, petting its long black snout. He lifted the shovel up as high as he could, standing up on his tippy-toes. The dragon kept a keen focus on it, and as its head tilted up, its rear end hit the ground. "Yes, goooood sit," Ashton said, then let the dragon nibble on one end of the shovel.

The dragon calmed. Ashton stroked behind the little gray horns protruding from the top of its head, and one of its hind legs pattered softly against the earth.

"See, nothing to be scared of," he said to Zetta. "We need to give it a name."

"We are not naming that thing," Zetta said. She remembered what her aunt had said about naming the rabbits. She didn't want to get attached to the dragon. Eventually, Aunt Meryl would return home and she would have to send it back to wherever it was supposed to be.

Zetta came out from behind the tree. Rift emerged from behind his boulder. Rayne decided to stay perched in the precariously standing tree, bow at the ready.

"I don't understand," Zetta said. "How did it grow so fast?"

Ashton shrugged. "It's hard to say, but I bet it molted. Its scales are still damp. There isn't exactly a lot of documentation on the ender dragon. And I'm kind of certain the endermen don't keep a lot of archives in the End."

"The end of what?" Rift asked.

"*The* End. One of the portal worlds. It's where endermen come from." Ashton took out his notebook and flipped it open to a page that said *What I know about the End* in big block letters, and below, in smaller script:

> *Where endermen come from*
> *Has no water*
> *Surrounded by void space (watch where you step!)*
> ~~*Possibly*~~ *home of a creature called the ender dragon*
> *End cities??? (Reed says he thinks I can get elytra there*
> *   so I can fly. I really want to fly!)*

Zetta stared at the little sketch below the list of Ashton soaring through the sky with wings on his back, kind of like that cape Aunt Meryl had worn. Then she slammed the book shut and shoved it back at Ashton. His imagination was getting out of hand.

The End sounded like a nightmare. Endermen freaked Zetta out big-time. How they just blinked from one place to another without regard to space and time. The friends spotted them once in a while on the outskirts of town. They kept to themselves, mostly, though sometimes they helped themselves to interesting blocks. There was a legend in Sienna Dunes that an enderman had once run off with the town's only grass block, way back before Zetta was even born.

"I think I see something," Rayne said, still up in the tree. They pointed toward a clearing in the woods. Rift trotted over to where Rayne was pointing and then ducked behind a stone outcropping. Zetta couldn't see him anymore. A whole minute passed without him saying anything.

"Rift?" Zetta called. "Is everything all right?"

"Rarg!" Rift said from behind Zetta. She turned and saw another ender dragon behind her. She nearly screamed, but then beneath the thin shell of a dragon skin, she saw Rift, smiling mischievously.

"Punk!" Zetta shouted, punching him in the shoulder.

"Sorry. Couldn't resist. But isn't this cool? It's the molting Ashton was talking about." Rift laid it carefully on the ground. The smoky gray skin was thin and translucent and was cracked in some places, but mostly it held the shape of the baby dragon Zetta had seen hatch.

"'Creepy' is the word I would use," Zetta said, poking it with a stick. "How much bigger is this thing supposed to get?"

"Um . . ." Ashton said, stepping back and looking at the dragon, holding his arms out and framing the beast between his fingers, assessing it. "Judging by the size of those massive paws, I'd say big. Really big. I mean, it is a dragon. They aren't exactly known for being petite."

Rift dared to stand right next to Ashton in front of the dragon. He reached out a tentative hand and stroked its snout. He pulled his hand back still attached, so Zetta decided to try the same thing. The dragon snuffed when she reached her hand out, though, and turned its head away before she could pet it.

"Still a little sore about the cave?" she asked it. "No worries. I get it. But I did bring you new friends like I promised."

The ender dragon ignored her and went back to gnawing on the end of the shovel.

"Are you coming down?" Rift called up to Rayne, still in the tree. He punched another piece of wood out of the trunk. "You know, we could gather up a ton of wood and take it back to town. We could sell some to the blacksmith for her tool handles." He punched another piece from the tree.

"Stop that!" Rayne said, their voice trembling. "I'll be down in a bit. I've just . . . I've got such a good vantage up here, and I—"

"You're scared. Admit it," Rift said.

"Nope, not scared. Just cautious. Someone has to keep watch, you know. And I spotted that molted skin, so . . . you know. Hanging up here for now. And stuff."

Zetta smiled. Rayne was the bravest of them all, but somehow that wasn't so with this dragon.

"Yeah, keep an eye out," she said encouragingly. "And find a different tree to punch, Rift. We can't take the wood back, though. People might start asking questions about where we got it. But we can use it to build a shelter here. I think this clearing would be a good place for us to set up camp with the dragon. We've got good tree coverage for privacy, and nearby streams and food sources. Plus my aunt's place is close enough that I can keep an eye on it while she's gone."

So that evening, they planned everything out. They'd take shifts with the dragon so it wouldn't be by itself, with Zetta and Ashton taking the first shift and Rift and Rayne returning home.

"Look," Zetta said to Ashton. "I'm not going to even pretend to know anything about animals, especially ones that are supposed to be imaginary, so why don't you and the dragon just play together or something." Zetta took a seat where the clearing turned back into forest. She crossed her arms and watched as Ashton goofed off with the frisky beast. Zetta really needed to get back to her aunt's place to clean up the dragon's mess, but she didn't want to leave Ashton alone with the dragon.

He used the wooden shovel and heaps of praise to teach the dragon some simple tasks. In twenty minutes, it could sit on command and could stay for a whole forty-five seconds before the zoomies got the best of it and it had to chase Ashton around. Then Ashton started working on having the beast lie down, but every time he got the dragon nearly to the ground, it would stare Zetta in the eye and snuff at her.

"Um . . ." Ashton said with possibly the biggest grimace on his face that Zetta had ever seen. "I think it doesn't trust you enough to put itself in such a vulnerable position. Do you mind giving us a little more space?"

Zetta sighed. If only she could explain her motivations to the dragon, maybe it would forgive her for walling it up in the cave. But she needed to gather wood for their shelter anyway, since Rift had lost interest in punching trees as soon as it didn't involve terrorizing his sibling. So Zetta headed into the woods to give it a go, found a suitable tree, and struck it square in the trunk.

Ouch.

After Zetta had knocked down the second tree, her knuckles were completely splintered. She was starting to wish she'd asked Rift for a recipe to make an axe before he left. She wasn't used to working with wood.

They were lucky to find sticks in the desert, let alone a whole tree. She couldn't imagine how easy building would be back home if they had all this lumber at their disposal. Zetta constructed a basic shelter with two small bedrooms and a larger common area. She cobbled together a furnace as well and stoked it with some wood planks to keep the place toasty once the sun set. She'd task Rayne with hunting when it was their turn for a shift, but in the meantime, Zetta filled a chest with all the food and water she had on her.

From within the privacy of the rustic shack, she was able to spy on Ashton without spooking the dragon. Ashton would tell the dragon "Stay," then walk behind it and hide the shovel behind a tree, and the dragon would sniff it out. They had such a great bond already, which made Zetta a little jealous. She was the one who'd found the egg, after all, and accidentally cracked it. She was the one who'd braved the desert and the hostile woods to get to her aunt's house in the first place. Zetta rubbed the bee stings on her arm from when she'd first gone up the mountain. They still stung, but not as much as getting snuffed at over and over again by the dragon.

When it looked like Ashton needed a breather, Zetta headed back out to offer him the last slice of Aunt Meryl's pumpkin pie. As she neared, she heard her cousin saying, "Where's Meechie? Where's Meechie?" in that cute, high-pitched voice.

"Meechie?" Zetta asked. "I thought we agreed we weren't going to name the dragon."

"Don't worry, Meechie is the shovel," Ashton said. "We named it."

"We?" Zetta said.

Ashton winked at the dragon. The dragon flared its nostrils and grunted like an out-of-tune horn. "It's an inside joke. Oh, is that pie for me?" He grabbed the slice before Zetta could answer and shoved it in his mouth.

"You're welcome," she said, watching as the crumbs tumbled down the front of his tunic.

"The dragon is so smart and willing to learn," Ashton said with a grin. "I think I could teach it anything!"

Zetta nodded. "Great. Teaching it not to destroy everything it touches would be a good start. I'm going to run up to Aunty Meryl's to check on the animals and clean up a bit." Zetta was now reasonably confident that the dragon wouldn't hurt Ashton. She wasn't quite as confident that Ashton wouldn't do anything foolish with the dragon, like try to ride on its back.

"Okay," Ashton said, barely paying her any attention. He was giving the dragon belly scritches.

Zetta sighed, then headed up the mountain, taking care to avoid the streams and beehives and a dozen other small but annoying nuisances, until she returned to her aunt's homestead. She fed the chickens and rabbits, making sure she locked the gate securely as she entered and exited the pen. Then she started cleaning up the mess the dragon had made, scrubbing the surfaces and arranging everything nice and neat. Too nice and neat.

Instead of the old and slightly enchanted place, it now looked like the inside of a furniture shop, everything so perfect that it sucked away all the personality. Zetta went around putting all the odds and ends back slightly askew. In one of the chests, she found some cobwebs, so she hung them up strategically in places. She dirtied the windows so she could barely see out of them. She ground dirt into the floorboards. Slowly, the place started to have more of a quirky atmosphere. This was the kind of place her aunt could brew in.

This was the kind of place Zetta could brew in, too.

If she were into that sort of thing anymore.

She shouldn't be into that sort of thing anymore.

Right?

She had successfully made that strength potion. And she and

her friends could really use some swiftness potions to help them get to town and back.

Zetta stared at the brewing stand that was the least damaged. Some of the blaze powder had fused to the sides of the intake valve, but it didn't seem completely clogged. Just a smidge of powder was left. Maybe it would be enough to make a few potions. It was worth a try at least.

Zetta took her empty potion bottles and washed them off in the cauldron before filling them with water and setting them in the brewing stand.

She knew it'd be more efficient to make them splash potions, but Zetta didn't dare chance using gunpowder again. Instead, she tossed some nether wart into the stand and waited for it to bubble up nicely. Then she carefully turned the burners down as low as they went before measuring in the sugar precisely. She watched the potions closely so they wouldn't caramelize, and when the time came, she sprinkled in a bit of redstone dust that she'd gotten from Rift.

And then . . .

The potions were done. Zetta let them cool, then took them off the stand. She stared at them. It had almost been too easy. Nothing had burnt or bubbled over. Nothing had exploded. She corked each bottle, then packed them up, then repeated the process again. She got six potions out of the stand before it finally died. Satisfied with her progress, Zetta headed back down the mountain to find Ashton and the dragon curled up next to a campfire, both sleeping.

"Isn't that cute?" Rift said from behind her. Zetta startled. The twins must have gotten back while she was gone.

"Super-cute," she said. "They worked really hard today."

"I've got something for you," Rift said.

Zetta smiled. It wasn't like Rift to be thoughtful, but then from the look on his face, she realized it was something she probably didn't want. He pulled out a piece of paper, folded twice in half. Her name was written on it in a familiar script. Her father's.

"He heard you'd been back to town. Someone saw you with us. I guess we weren't careful enough." Rift shrugged. "He asked me to give this to you."

Zetta's arms wouldn't leave her sides. She didn't want it. Didn't want to know what it said. She could already imagine. After spending several moments with the note outstretched in his arm, Rift came closer and pressed it into Zetta's hand. It felt heavy, much heavier than paper should be, but Zetta knew it was because the words written upon it would weigh so heavily on her heart.

She balled it up and tossed it into the campfire.

Rift's eyes went wide. "Zetta—"

"It's fine. I'll talk to him when I get back. You didn't tell him about the dragon, did you?" she asked.

"Of course not!"

Zetta breathed a deep sigh of relief, but before she could get it fully out, Rift continued.

"But I did tell him about your aunt's place."

Fire surged through Zetta's veins. "You what?" she screamed.

Rift backed up and threw his hands out in front of him like he thought Zetta was about to attack. Maybe she was. "I had to tell him something!" he stammered. "To explain why you were gone so long. To explain where we were going!"

"You could have made something up!" Zetta said. "Anything! Gathering more dirt blocks to expand the farm or looking for bigger lakes to fish in or finding flowers to help decorate for the Eve of Hostile Mobs." She'd almost have preferred it if Rift had told her father about the dragon instead. Almost.

"Well, I'm not as good at lying as you are, apparently," Rift said with a huff.

The fire within Zetta went cold, and suddenly she found herself shivering with fury. "What's that supposed to mean?"

Rift's mouth trembled, like he wanted to say more but realized he shouldn't.

"What's with all the shouting?" Ashton asked, rubbing the sleep from his eyes. "Is my shift over?"

Zetta blinked a few times, then turned to look at her cousin, managing to scrape a smile onto her face in the couple of seconds that passed. "Hey, yeah. Rift and Rayne are here to take over. Where is Rayne, anyway?"

"'Assessing the perimeter for hostiles' is what they said. I think Rayne's still nervous about being around the dragon, if you ask me." Rift rolled his eyes. "But we've got great plans. Not going to share them now. It'll be a surprise for when you get back in the morning."

"Speaking of which," Zetta said, looking at the sun starting to set in the sky. "We'd better get going. I found some swiftness potions at my aunt's place." She downed a potion, then handed one to her cousin, the truth pressed at the back of her teeth. Technically, she *had* found them in the brewing stand after she'd brewed them.

Rift's words came back at her. Was she a good liar? She was certainly crafty with the truth, omitting pieces here and there. But if she told everyone that she'd brewed the potions herself, no one would want to use them. Not after the incident with the mayor.

The truth was, like it or not, Rift was right.

"Ashton," Zetta said, as his lips pressed to the bottle. "Wait—"

She was having second thoughts, but the kid was already guzzling down her swiftness potion like he'd been chugging them his whole life. He wiped away the blue stain above his lip with the back of his arm, then let out the tiniest burp.

"I could drink ten of those," Ashton said. "It's sweeter than cake!"

"One is plenty," Zetta said, grimacing. She felt fine herself. She was sure everything would be okay. When Ashton returned the bottle, however, his overeager lopsided smile had been replaced with a concerned look.

"You okay?" Zetta asked.

"Yeah. Just nervous about leaving the dragon," Ashton said, glancing at the still snoring beast. "We'd better go before it wakes up and sees me. It'll be easier to leave that way."

Zetta nodded, unsure if Ashton meant easier for the dragon or easier for him. Probably both. Ashton handed Meechie the shovel to Rift with the solemn gesture of passing on a scepter to a new king, then flashed a wan smile.

"The dragon is in good hands," Rift said, patting Ashton on the shoulder. "Don't worry a single bit. See you in the morning!"

And with that, Zetta and Ashton were off. Running, running, running. With each step, Zetta gained just a tiny bit more confidence in her belief that maybe one day she really could be a great potioner. Or alchemist, as her aunt Meryl called it.

The sun started to set before they could make it all the way to town, so they drank another set of potions to enable them to rush past all the mobs that started to gather around dusk. The odd arrow shot in their direction, but none ever came close to hitting them. As the familiar bell tower came into Zetta's view, the dread of dealing with mobs was replaced with the dread of dealing with her father.

CHAPTER
ELEVEN

After walking Ashton home, Zetta returned to the safety of the barn rafters. Hunger was burning in the pit of her stomach, but she was so nervous that she didn't dare try to see if she could keep food down. Plus, the sugar from the second swiftness potion she'd guzzled still had her jumpy. She'd return home to see her father. She just needed to calm herself first, so Zetta laid her head down on a pile of hay for a minute.

As soon as her lids shut, they popped back open, but it was light out, with the sun peeking through the barn's wooden slats. Oh no. She'd actually gone to sleep. She'd have to set out to relieve Rift and Rayne soon, and she didn't want to be late. But she absolutely couldn't leave again before talking to her father.

Zetta rushed home, hoping to catch him before he left for his mining shift. She got there just as he was closing the front door. He stopped when he saw her, standing still, looking like a statue. "Zetta," he uttered. His disappointment was beyond evident in the way he said her name. He really didn't need to say anything else.

"I'm sorry I left without telling you where I was going," Zetta blurted out. "But I'm not sorry for going. I needed to talk to Aunty Meryl. I needed to learn about potioning from someone who knows what they're doing."

Father's brow stiffened at the mention of Aunt Meryl's name, and the creases on his irritable face deepened further when Zetta said the word "potioning."

"Magical nonsense isn't going to save—"

"Don't worry, she wouldn't teach me anything. Mostly because she didn't want to upset you. But she did tell me about Mom. About the wither. Why didn't you ever tell me?" Zetta asked.

Father shook his head. "That's not what we're talking about right now. We're discussing your responsibilities and your lack of respect for me and for the bylaws of this town. We don't do magic here. You saw what you did to the mayor!"

"I scared off a ravager that was about to trample her. I think Mayor Maxine could deal with having an invisible head for a few hours rather than having it knocked off completely!"

"A few days is more like it," her father grumbled. "The spell took forever to wear off. Whatever you did—"

Zetta snickered. She didn't mean to, but all the tension and anxiety bubbling up inside her had to go somewhere, and thinking about the mayor going around as a disembodied torso for three days just made her giggle. And once she started, she couldn't stop. "I'm sorry," she said to her father, holding the stitch in her side with one hand and wiping the tears in her eyes away with the other. "I'm sorry. I'm not laughing at you. I'm . . ." She took a deep breath. "I'm okay. I'm fine."

She wasn't, but she needed to pretend to be so she could get through this conversation and get back to the dragon.

"I'm just watching over Aunty Meryl's place while she's gone anyway, not doing any magic." Lie.

"She's got tons of animals that need to be tended to, so I recruited Rift and Rayne to help out. And Ashton." Another lie.

"We're being really careful and avoiding hostile mobs at all costs." Big ole lie.

There was one scaly, black-winged mob that they were definitely not avoiding. Cute and cuddly now, but they couldn't forget that it was indeed hostile.

The lies came so easily. They rolled off her tongue so effortlessly. Zetta tried to tell herself that this was all for the good of her people, but she couldn't help but wonder if there was a better way. Maybe, but she didn't have time to figure that out right now.

"I've got to get going," Zetta told her father. "You're always telling me to be more responsible. I promised Aunty Meryl, so . . ."

Zetta's father looked deflated, and she started feeling bad about misleading him, but then she reminded herself that he was keeping secrets about her mother, so maybe this made them even. She kept her eye contact firm, not willing to back down from her lie, until finally, her father relented. "Fine. But you can't ignore your responsibilities in the mine. You'll have to pull those shifts as well."

"But—"

"No buts. You should have taken that into account before you made promises that you'd have trouble keeping."

Zetta looked at the rising sun, still low in the sky. She could squeeze in half a shift now and do the rest when she was back this weekend. So she'd have to give up a few hours of sleep to tend to all her responsibilities, but it would be worth it in the end, when they had the dragon trained not to be so destructive.

Zetta ran back to her cousin's place to tell him that she'd be running a little late, but then her grandpa caught sight of her and invited her in for his famous baked potatoes. And, well, Zetta couldn't say no. Oh, she *wanted* to say no, but then Papa would get all fussy and go on a rant about how in his day, his parents didn't even have two sticks to rub together to make a campfire and fed him nothing but raw potatoes, how he would have given his very soul to the nether to have a fine baked potato like this.

And then Nana would give Papa that impatient look of hers, and say something like, "Now Noah Night, how many times do I have to tell you that nobody cares about your potatoes?" And Papa would get huffy and mutter "Someday, they'll care, Livvie. You'll see . . ." under his breath, and then he'd pout for the rest of the day. Meals at the farm were always a bit dramatic.

So Zetta stuffed a few bites in her mouth, hoping her queasy stomach wouldn't violently object, then she was on her way to the mines. She arrived just as Milo, her mining partner, did. Not late. Not technically. She cleared her throat loudly as she walked past her father to make sure that he saw her. He was the type who'd say if you're ten minutes early, you're on time, and if you're on time, you're late. He'd probably collected several stacks of terracotta already, but that wasn't Zetta's concern. She took out her pickaxe and got to work.

"You look distracted," Milo said as he and Zetta started mining in their section. He slammed his sleek iron pickaxe down on a block of yellow terracotta until it popped free. Milo was one of the town's best miners, and he had the most luck coming across ores.

He'd called first rights to nearly twenty iron veins in the past few months, which meant he'd been given the first ore he'd discovered, while the rest were hauled off to the town vault. Milo had a nice iron pickaxe to show for it. With it, he could dig deeper and have a better chance at coming across more valuable ores: gold, lapis, diamonds . . .

"Well, I'm not distracted," Zetta replied grumpily. The night had passed so quickly that it felt like she hadn't slept at all, and her nerves were still shot from dealing with the dragon.

"Just watch where you're swinging that axe," Milo said. Today's shift had just started, and his cropped, pale blond hair had already turned bright yellow from terracotta dust. His cheeks were flushed from exertion and he had an intense focus on his face. He wasn't going to let Zetta distract him from a solid day's mining.

Zetta ignored him and moved over a dozen blocks and started a mining section of her own. She slammed her stone pickaxe down again and again. Her thoughts were gnawing at her. Had she locked her aunt's door when she left? Had she turned off the burner on the brewing stand? Were the animals okay? She'd closed the gate, right?

In her worry, Zetta had done the first thing she'd been taught not to do as a miner—dig straight down. She tried to stop herself mid-swing, but the momentum carried through, and the block beneath her crumbled to bits. Seconds later, the dark shaft was filled with bright, red light.

Lava. Zetta stuck her hands and feet out, holding on for dear life as the heat made its way up, slowly blistering her skin. "Help!" she yelled up the shaft, hoping she wasn't so far down that Milo wouldn't hear her. Her hands were sweating and starting to lose grip.

"Coming!" said Milo's voice from the top of the shaft. Zetta hoped that he'd rescue her without a lot of fuss, but he'd started yelling to the others that she was in trouble. Zetta cringed. Milo was right. She had been distracted. Now every single miner would know how badly she'd messed up.

Finally, Milo started stacking ladders down toward her. But as Zetta looked up, she saw the light of the lava illuminating a block that she'd missed in the dark. Gold ore.

Big flecks of gold glimmered in the lava's warm glow. Zetta never mined this far down. She didn't have the experience or the right pickaxe to break through the more precious ores, and more importantly, she hadn't been cleared for this type of mining by her father. Now she was never going to hear the end of it, but while she was down here, she might as well make the claim and get her first rights.

"Thanks, Milo," she said as he got closer. "I know I messed up, but I think I discovered a gold vein. Can I borrow your pickaxe?"

Despite the trouble she knew she was about to get into, Zetta was excited.

"Don't worry about the gold," Milo said. "We need to get you out of here." His voice was trembling. She'd never seen him like this; Milo was always so sure of himself. Suddenly the gravity of having a bubbling lava lake right below her sunk in. Zetta wanted nothing more than to get out of this hole as quickly as possible. She climbed up the ladder as soon as it was close enough, then headed back toward the surface. Zetta couldn't believe she'd mined down all that way, lost in thought.

She stopped when a familiar face popped into view.

"Dad," Zetta said.

"Zetta," he said, a sigh of resignation that said *Of course, it's my daughter* following closely after. Dad stretched his hand out to her, and she took it, feeling small and fragile in his grip, like she was a child again and he was helping her cross the busy town square. "I've got you."

"Thanks," Zetta mumbled.

"I guess I don't need to say that I'm disappointed in you," her father said, capping the hole with a block of red terracotta as soon as she and Milo were out. "You know better. Tell me what's really going on with you."

"Nothing, Dad. Just life."

"Look me in the eyes and say that again," he said.

Zetta realized that she was looking all over the place, in every direction except at her father. Her foot was tapping quickly.

A scowl crossed her father's face. "Zetta, I don't think you're taking this situation seriously. We need everyone on their best game out here so we can get the wall and watchtowers finished in time."

"Which watchtowers?" Zetta asked.

"If you hadn't run off, you would have heard the mayor's announcement. We're building four watchtowers into the wall to give us an early warning and a strategic advantage for our archers. Which means we need even more terracotta. We don't have time for you to be distracting everyone."

"It was a mistake, Dad. People make mistakes!" Zetta said. "I promise I'll do better. Now let me get back to—"

Zetta's father snatched the pickaxe out of her hand. "You're no longer a miner," he told her.

"What?" Zetta said. She'd wanted to hear those words for so long, but not like this. She felt like something was being taken from her instead of getting out of a task she loathed so much. "You can't do that!"

"I'm the mining manager for this shift. I can do what I want. We no longer need your help. Go home."

Zetta's lip trembled. "Okay," she said, trying to keep back the tears. Her father had always been bitter toward the whole world, but this felt different. It felt personal.

Zetta walked back to town, alone. As she approached, she saw the wall and the starts of watchtowers being built at the corners. She didn't understand why her father and all the other adults in town were being so stubborn. Why were they investing time in this wall, when they knew it hadn't worked the first time? Why couldn't they even entertain the idea that there might be better ways? And yeah, maybe watchtowers were an improvement, but wouldn't they be even better if the archers had poison-tipped arrows? Or if they could lob splash potions from up there as well?

Zetta wanted to believe that she could leave Sienna Dunes' protection to the adults, but they just weren't acting fast enough. They needed to be bolder. They needed to prepare for the worst, because who knew how big the next raid would be. And maybe Zetta messed up a lot, but her ideas were solid. She could contribute to the town in more ways than mining terracotta.

Her aunt Meryl's words ran through her head, about how Zetta's mother messed up a lot, too, and started keeping a journal. Dad kept some of Mother's old things in the hall closet. Maybe her journal was in there, too. She ran home, which felt like an alien place now. Drab sandstone lined all the surfaces, and a potted dead bush sat in the front window. Zetta couldn't remember it ever being alive.

An old music player sat in the corner. When she used to babysit Ashton, they'd toss on a record and dance for hours, but it had gone unused for so long now, Zetta wasn't sure if it even worked anymore. She saw how dank and desperate her home seemed compared to the warmth of her aunt's place. How were she and her father even related? They were so different. Or maybe tragedy just affected them in different ways.

Zetta opened the old chest in the hall closet. It was full of odds and ends—an old saddle, a broken fishing pole, and old music discs. All this junk hinted at the person her father had once been, before he'd folded up into himself. She took out a disc and stuck it into the player in the living room. Zetta thought she'd get a taste of some old-timey music, but was surprised to hear her dad and aunt singing a silly duet together. Goofing off. And if there was one thing that her father didn't do, it was goof off. Still, it made Zetta smile as they harmonized, their lyrics all about desert life — half complaining, half celebrating.

> Who needs grass when you've got sand?
> With cactus growin' 'cross the land?
> The desert sun, she burns so bright.
> Our days are hot, but cool's the night.
> Oak trees are rare, and so's the rain.
> I'm never leavin', what's the gain?
> Life mightn't go the way you planned,
> But who needs grass when you've got sand?

Zetta bobbed her head as she continued to dig through the chest. It was completely crammed, and since there wasn't a torch in the closet, it was difficult to see the stuff down at the bottom. So Zetta pulled the chest out into the living room where she could get more light. Stone buttons. A bunch of crumbly coal. Some dried-up beet root seeds. A lead that had lost its stretch. A pile of lime green dye . . .

No notebook. Just a bunch of useless stuff.

Zetta sighed, then started humming to herself as she dragged the chest back into the closet. "Who needs grass when you've got—"

The closet's wood floor creaked loudly as she stepped on it. It was odd enough that the floor was made from wood—most of the house had sandstone flooring, with patches of carpet for softness and warmth. But then Zetta noticed that one of the wood blocks was different from the others, more like a little door than flooring. She jiggled at it, pushed it, tried to pull it, but it wouldn't open. She remembered seeing a button in the chest, so she dug through and found it and then placed it next to the little wooden door.

She pressed it. It opened.

Zetta stepped back. Why did her father have this secret door? She gathered her courage and peeked down inside. There was another chest, and of course Zetta had to open it. Her eyes lit up when she saw her brewing stand. Her father would be furious if she took it and he noticed it was gone, but she could remove the blaze powder to use back at her aunt's place.

Zetta emptied the powder into her pack, but as she put the brewing stand back, something else in the chest caught her attention—a notebook with the word *"Inventions"* scribbled across the leather cover.

Zetta knew it was her mother's handwriting. This had to be what she'd been looking for. She took the book out and slowly flipped through the pages. Written in very delicate script were instructions for building various mechanical contraptions. Intricate diagrams accompanied the writing, including depictions of the whole contraption as well as up-close details and cross sections. There were several designs for piston doors, a device for automatically sorting stored items, a slime block catapult . . .

She stopped when she got to the page titled "Wither Destroyer."

It was huge, much larger than she'd imagined. The instructions went on for sixteen pages, starting with an inventory of each and every block needed for the construction.

"My mother was a genius," Zetta whispered to herself.

Seconds later, she heard the front door open. Her father was home early. Zetta stuffed the book into her pack, then hit the button so hard the trapdoor snapped with a loud crack that echoed through their house. Oh no. There was no way her father hadn't heard that. She worked quickly, shoving the chest back in place. Ah, the music disc! She ran to the music player and took the disc out, but her father arrived in the room before she could return it.

"Zetta?" he said, looking at the open closet, then back at her.

Zetta wanted to wipe the sweat from her brow, but she didn't want to appear more guilty than she was.

"Hey, Dad. Just tidying up a bit. Look what I found." She showed him the disc, hoping beyond hope that he'd be happy to see it, or at least be distracted enough not to ask a whole lot of questions as to what she was doing.

"Where'd you get that?" he snapped.

"In the chest there. It was a little dusty so—"

Her father grabbed the disc. For a moment, Zetta thought he was going to break it in half, but a deep frown crossed over his face as he stared at it. He went back into the closet and shoved the disc into the chest. "Don't go in here again," he said gruffly. "Understand?"

Zetta nodded. "Sorry about today," she said. "You were right. I should have been paying more attention."

Her father sighed, then tossed Zetta a gold ingot and an iron one. "First rights," he said.

Zetta's eyes lit up.

"That gold ore you discovered led to eight more. And half a dozen blocks of iron ore. We haven't had a vein that productive in months." Her father shuffled his feet. "This doesn't make what you did any more right. Digging straight down is dangerous. You could have fallen into that lava."

"I know, Dad. It won't happen again."

"I know it won't. We're starting a new round of mining training next week. You'll have to take it again before you're left unsupervised with a pickaxe."

"Okay," Zetta said sheepishly. She couldn't believe that she actually felt relief to get another shot at mining. Maybe it was the taste of gold in her hands. Maybe it was some deep need to have a chance to redeem herself in her father's eyes. But then she felt the weight of the notebook in her pack. How was her father supposed to trust her ever again if she was keeping everything that mattered from him?

Still, she knew the risk in telling him about the dragon.

The air between Zetta and her father thickened, like he was waiting for her to spill her soul.

She wanted to. But she couldn't. This was too important.

The truth would have to wait.

CHAPTER
TWELVE

Zetta struggled to keep pace with Ashton, even after downing a swiftness potion. The kid was a natural sprinter, jumping up and down to go even faster in a way that made Zetta tired just from watching him. She wanted to stop and lie down for a few minutes. Or a few hours. Between the bad sleep, the stress of dealing with the dragon the day before, nearly scorching herself in lava on her mining shift, and the shock of discovering her mother's journal, she was completely overwhelmed.

But there was no time to rest.

When they arrived at the clearing, Zetta was so cranky and disoriented that she couldn't make out Rift's excited banter. He'd done something. Crafted something great. He pulled Zetta and Ashton over to a mechanical contraption of some sort.

"What is it?" Ashton asked.

Rift bobbed his brows. "You know how the dragon makes you throw Meechie over and over and over and over and ov—"

"Yeah, we get it," Zetta snapped. "So what?"

"Well, I've solved all of our problems!" Rift took a shovel from the chest—not Meechie, just a plain wooden shovel without the face drawn on it. "All you have to do is drop the shovel in here, and . . ." Rift placed the shovel into a hopper, and red dust lit up all around it. Zetta heard a bunch of clicking, and then finally, the shovel shot out from the dispenser and into the woods.

"Cool!" Ashton said.

"I even taught the dragon to bring the shovel back and place it into the hopper. It was really excited. And then I just sat back and watched as the dragon chased Meechie and returned it to the contraption, over and over and over and over and over and ov—"

Zetta cleared her throat, rolled her eyes, then gave Ashton a look that said, *See, I told you that everything would be okay.*

"I had a bunch of extra time on my hands, I guess." Rift shrugged. "How did things go with your father?"

"They went," Zetta said, pulling out her mother's notebook. "But I did discover something I think you'll really like. Gather around, everyone."

Rift, Zetta, and Ashton all sat on a log near the campfire upwind of the little puffs of smoke. Rayne sauntered over from the nearby stream, tossed some raw salmon onto the fire, but didn't sit down. Though Rayne never said anything to alarm the friends about potential threats, Zetta knew Rayne's reluctance to let their guard down around camp was because there were so many hostile mobs lurking about in the forest. Zetta tried to forget about that and flipped the notebook open to the page with the wither destroyer.

"Whoa," Ashton said, leaning in to look at the illustration. A sketch of the wither sat in the middle of the contraption, with dozens of arrows and potions flying at it.

"Why are the arrowheads all different colors?" Rayne asked, leaning in as well.

Zetta flipped to the next page, which detailed the arrows used and the types of magic they possessed. "The arrows are dipped in potions," Zetta said to Rayne.

"I didn't even know that was possible," they said, swiping the hair out of their face to see better. "Imagine being able to poison our enemy from a hundred feet away!"

"Yes!" Zetta said. "And my aunt told me that my mother built this contraption to slay a wither. Maybe Rift could build something similar to help out with the illagers!"

Zetta looked over at Rift, who was sitting at the edge of the log, arms crossed over his chest.

"Yeah, no. That looks way too complicated. And I'm more of a 'make pranks, not war' kind of guy."

Zetta nudged Rift in the shoulder. "This is your chance to contribute something useful to the town! You've got a great brain. You need to use it for good. Like your shovel thrower! It's amazing that you thought of the dragon's needs."

"Yeah, that did feel pretty nice," Rift mumbled. "And Rayne helped me adjust the aim. I guess I can take a look at the notebook. Maybe there's something in there that's a little more my speed."

"This calls for a celebration," Rayne said, taking out a melon and handing out slices to everyone. "Look what we found growing nearby."

Zetta looked back and forth between the twins, a huge grin on her face. Now they were starting to feel like a proper team, and sharing a juicy melon would be a great way to celebrate. "I've got to admit, Ashton and I were a little worried to leave you with the dragon, but we shouldn't have been. You both did an amazing job! Right, Ashton?"

"Yeah. . . ." Ashton said, about to take a bite of melon when he suddenly started looking around. "Um, y'all, where's the dragon?" he asked.

"Gone after Meechie, I told you," Rift said. "It's been chasing it back and forth, over and over and—"

"I get that. But shouldn't it have been back by now?" Ashton asked. "This contraption can't possibly throw *that* far . . ."

Rift looked blankly at Rayne, then said, "I guess it's been a while since we actually saw the dragon bring Meechie back."

The gleeful mood that had filled the woods a few moments before was replaced by a quiet chill. The friends all looked back and forth between one another. Zetta's stomach went sour. She packed the melon slice away and took a deep breath.

"You lost the dragon," Zetta accused Rift and Rayne.

"No we didn't! It's around here somewhere," Rift said. "Come on, let's go look."

The friends ventured into the woods, the leaves brushing against Zetta's cheeks as they got deeper and deeper. Fortunately, the dragon left behind so many busted-up tree trunks and dirt gouges that the friends could follow without a problem. They went uphill, the woods getting denser and darker, and even though the sun was still high in the sky, all the shadows around them meant they had to keep an eye out for zombies and skeletons and—

"Creeper! On the right!" Rayne said, stepping back and drawing an arrow into their bow. Right as the mob started flickering white, about to explode, Rayne unleashed four arrows in fast succession. The creature poofed, leaving nothing behind but a pile of gunpowder.

"Nice," Rift said, going to pick up the powder, but Zetta stepped in and took it instead.

"Not trusting you with gunpowder. Can't even trust you to take care of a baby dragon," Zetta said, like she was one to talk. But who knew what Rift could get up to with that kind of power in his pranks.

"This way," Ashton said, eager to get back to tracking the dragon down.

Zetta followed her cousin along, sword drawn. She heard a shuffling off in the woods, some mob walking through the underbrush, too close to leave untended. It could circle back behind and ambush them if they weren't careful.

"I'm going to check it out," Zetta said. "Back in a sec."

"I'm coming with you," Rayne said, bow drawn.

As they got closer, they heard two sets of feet moving. Rayne and Zetta looked at each other, unsure. They could take out two zombies, right? Zetta held her hand up, counted to three, then rapidly cut through the dense foliage so they'd have the element of surprise.

Staring at her were two giant black nostrils. At first, she thought it was the dragon, but when she pulled back, she saw it was just a cow.

Just a cow?

Zetta's mind started churning. If she brought a cow back to town to replace the one they'd lost in the raid, everyone would have to forgive her for turning the mayor half invisible. Maybe they'd forget about her little lava adventure, too. She lunged for the stunned beast, but it was already spooked and started trotting off in the opposite direction.

"Help me catch it!" she said to Rayne, who was no better with animals than she was. Zetta thought about screaming for Ashton to come join them, but figured yelling would only startle the cow further.

If only she had some wheat on her, she could lure it back to camp.

After a short chase, Zetta and Rayne had the cow cornered. It mooed angrily at them. What was it even doing in the forest, anyway? Zetta didn't ponder the question. This was her chance.

A sharp whistle cut through the air.

Rayne perked. "That's Rift," they said, voice heavy with concern.

Zetta listened, and could just barely hear Rift calling out their names.

"He needs us," Rayne said. "Now."

"But the cow!" Zetta said.

"We can come back for it."

Zetta sighed. She knew they'd never find the cow again if they left now. She started punching a nearby tree. "Maybe I can make a fence so it doesn't wander—"

Zetta heard Ashton's scream next, and the hairs on the back of her neck stood on end. In the next moment, they were both running through the woods the way they'd come. They shouldn't have split up. They shouldn't have chased after the cow. Instead of thinking about herself, Zetta should have been thinking about the safety of the team. She would never forgive herself if something bad happened to her cousin or Rift.

Finally, they made it back out to the main path. They kept running, following the footprints in the wet dirt.

"Rift! Ashton!" Rayne called out into the dense woods. But there was no response.

Finally, they spotted Ashton and Rift, shuffling slowly along the path, arms to their sides. The canopy above was so thick here that it only let in traces of sunlight, and yet purple light shone from every direction, blinking in and out like twinkling stars. Weird. Even weirder, Ashton and Rift kept staring at the ground. As her eyes began to adjust to the shadows, Zetta realized why.

There were endermen. Everywhere. At least twenty of the tall, black figures teleporting back and forth with no rhyme or reason.

Some held grass blocks in their too-long arms. One of them nearly made eye contact with Zetta, but she quickly turned her head, only to lock eyes with the enderman standing not three feet away from her.

Its mouth opened wide, its jaw unhinging like an angry jack-o'-lantern's, and the most spine-chilling shriek came out. Then it lunged at Zetta and struck her in the arm, a sharp attack that felt much like a bee sting, except that the feeling jolted through her whole body.

It felt as if her brain had reset for half a second, and by the time she swung her sword at the enderman, it was gone. Then it was on her other side, its piercing scream scraping against her right eardrum this time. Another strike hit her. This one to the temple.

"Run!" Ashton shouted. "Straight ahead. I can hear the dragon."

Zetta thought it'd be best to turn around and go back the way they came, but the enderman punched her in the mouth, and then her jaw was too sore to open to say something, so she ran. She couldn't take too many more hits like that. Not when her only armor was a pair of rabbit-hide boots.

The woods started to thin. Zetta thought she could see something big and black in the clearing beyond. Definitely the dragon. It didn't look like it normally did, though. It was breathing slowly, hunched over, almost like it was in pain. Zetta had made a point not to get too attached to the beast, but seeing it like this made her want to run over and comfort it.

But as the friends neared the dragon, enderman after enderman zapped in from nowhere, blocking their path. The endermen were acting so weird. Then all at once, they started screaming, a chorus out of a nightmare. The friends put their hands to their ears, then turned and bolted back toward camp.

The sounds of teleporting mobs were right on their heels for several minutes, but no one looked back.

CHAPTER THIRTEEN

The friends ran and ran until they were all locked up safe inside their little shack in the woods.

"What the heck was that?" Zetta scolded her cousin. "You can't sneak your way through a flock of endermen! What if . . . what if . . ." She couldn't even get the words out. What if he'd been killed?

"We were doing fine until you showed up," Rift snapped. "We had it under control."

"Now the dragon is out there all alone. We have to go back," Ashton said.

Zetta shook her head. "We are not going back. The dragon is fine. It can take care of itself, and in any case, it's definitely not alone. What was with those endermen? It was like they were guarding it."

"We shouldn't have split up," Rayne said. "You had us chasing cows when we should have had Rift's and Ashton's backs."

"Well, maybe if you were a better shot," Zetta huffed, "then you could have taken out the pillager that shot our cow in the first place!"

Rift stepped in. "Same shot that killed the raider that was about to mow you down with an axe? Curious. I didn't see you complaining about Rayne's aim then."

"I don't need this stress," Rayne said. "We've got enough going on trying to fortify the town and rebuild. Some of us actually care that our people are safe."

"Yeah," Rift agreed. "We quit."

Rift and Rayne started packing their bags in a huff. Zetta's eyes were hot in their sockets, a mixture of anger and wanting to cry over her friends' cruel words. She knew she couldn't let them leave, though. Not angry like this. If Sienna Dunes was to have a chance, the friends needed to stick together and not be at one another's throats. She saw so much potential in what they could accomplish. She was slowly getting better with potions. Rift was skilled with redstone contraptions. And Rayne had the best aim and a natural curiosity about using magic to improve how weapons worked.

As much as Zetta loved Sienna Dunes, she knew it wouldn't be able to remain caught in the past. The world was changing all around them. Zetta and her friends were changing with it. They needed to get the rest of the town on board, just like her mother and aunt had tried to do so many years ago. Only now, they couldn't afford to fail.

"Wait!" Zetta shouted. "I'm sorry. I didn't mean any of that. It's just, I'm on edge. We all are. We want to protect our town more than anything. What if . . . what if we started small?" She took out her mother's notebook and flipped through it. "We don't have to do something like a wither destroyer. Maybe this arrow-slinging contraption would do fine. Or here's a TNT cannon."

Rift stopped packing and turned around. "A TNT cannon?" he asked.

Rift grabbed the notebook from Zetta, and his eyes went wide. "So much TNT," he mumbled, flipping from page to page. "Looks complicated. But not impossible."

"Do you think you could make it?" Zetta asked, pleased that she'd lured her friend back so easily. Maybe their friendship wasn't so fragile after all.

Rift nodded slowly. "I'll gather the materials and we can test it out here, in the woods."

"That's probably smart. Plus, maybe we can take a shot with the arrow-slinging contraption, too," Rayne added, hopeful. "We've got plenty of hostile mobs as neighbors out here, and we could use a little extra defense."

"Yeah, yeah . . ." Rift muttered, already lost in thought as he scribbled in his own notebook.

Not soon after, he and Rayne were gone for the evening. Ashton and Zetta were left in the hut, staring at each other.

"The dragon will be fine," Zetta said.

"You don't know that," Ashton said, voice angry and cracking around the edges.

They stared at each other in silence. At some point, Zetta must have dozed off, because soon the sun was rising again, and from its angle in the sky, she knew she'd be late to work, even if she took her last swiftness potion.

A strange huffing noise was coming from right outside their hut. Ashton woke at it, too, then he sat straight up.

"The dragon!" he screamed. "It came back!" He got up and ran out the front door. Zetta followed on wobbly legs, and she was still wiping the sleep out of her eyes when she ran right into Ashton.

"Why'd you stop right in the middle of the—" She shook her head and looked at the dragon before them. It was bigger again. Much, much bigger. The cute puppy dog eyes were gone, replaced with a menacing stare sitting under heavy brows.

"It molted again," Ashton said, raising his hand toward the dragon and creeping forward.

"Ashton, I swear if you take another step—" Zetta started, but it was too late. Her cousin was already patting the dragon's snout. Its tail thudded against the ground, sending a large tremor that knocked the dispenser off Rift's shovel launcher. All the shovels tumbled out suddenly, spooking the dragon. It flapped its enormous wings, air gushing past Zetta's face so hard, she had to close her eyes. By the time she opened them again, the dragon was airborne.

"That is so cool," Ashton said, eyes turned up to the sky. "I wonder if it'll let me—"

"You will not ride that thing. Promise me that, Ashton. I'm serious. You cannot put yourself in that kind of danger."

"Statistically, I'm pretty sure riding on the back of an ender dragon is the safest way to travel. Who's going to mess with you?"

Zetta didn't want to admit it, but the kid had a point. She shook her head. "Who needs to worry about endermen? Nana and Papa are going to poof me themselves when they find out that I've got you up on a dragon."

"So . . . you'll let me ride?" Ashton asked. As if on cue, the dragon dipped down from the treetops and landed gently in front of him. The beast's chest puffed out, like it was so proud of itself.

They couldn't keep the dragon here forever, not with all those endermen lurking about. Zetta was ready to consider moving the dragon closer to home, and being able to fly the dragon would make that a lot easier. She sighed. "Okay, but you have to be super careful. No fancy stunts, and you have to keep both hands on the dragon at all times."

"Awesome," Ashton said, hopping up and down. "Just let me work with the dragon for a bit. I ride the pigs on the farm all the time! How much different could it be?"

"Right," Zetta said in a peppy voice, trying to instill some confidence into her cousin, but truth was, she was terrified. Riding a three-ton winged beast through the sky was a whole lot different than riding a hungry pig chasing after a carrot on a fishing pole. If Ashton slipped . . .

He wouldn't slip. Ashton trusted the dragon and the dragon trusted Ashton. In thirty minutes Ashton would probably be riding through the clouds, and Zetta would be laughing at how ridiculous she'd been to worry about such things.

Zetta watched closely as Ashton climbed up onto the dragon's back.

"All right, come on. Take off! Up in the sky with you!" he said.

The dragon turned its attention to pawing a divot into the dirt.

"Don't be shy!" Ashton said, an encouraging lilt in his voice. "You can do it."

The dragon huffed.

"Giddyap!" Ashton scratched his head. "Is that what you say to fly, or is that just horses?"

"Both hands on the dragon," Zetta barked.

Ashton and the dragon cut their attention her way. The dragon's purple eyes eased into angry slits. If looks could kill . . .

Zetta gulped. Maybe they didn't need her oversight. She needed to check on the animals at Aunt Meryl's anyway. So Zetta made her way up to the little house, threw feed into all the pens, and tidied up some around the property, all while steering clear of the spooky porch and the haunted soul sand. When she was done, she made sure all the gates and doors were locked up tight, then started back down the mountain to check on her cousin.

She'd only taken a few strides when she heard flapping in the sky, like someone shaking out bedsheets. She looked up and saw the dragon overhead, Ashton on its neck, both hands thrown up in the sky, having the time of his life.

She vowed to give that kid a good talking-to about taking unnecessary risks, but before she could even form a single sentence in her head, the dragon swooped down so low that Zetta had to duck to avoid being decapitated by those sharp claws. The dragon landed gracefully behind her.

"Hop on, Zetta!" Ashton said. "Flying is easier than walking. No low-hanging branches or holes to look out for. Just an endless stretch of sky and no cares in the world!"

Gravity. Zetta cared about gravity, but she didn't say that out loud.

"Okay." She approached the dragon. It looked at her suspiciously, eyes narrowed. It huffed and jostled away from her when she tried to climb up. "Come on, you can't possibly still be holding a grudge."

Zetta tried to climb up again, but this time the dragon purposefully bumped her.

"Oh, Dragon, don't be like that," Ashton said, patting the base of the dragon's long neck. It turned back to look at him. "She's sorry. Aren't you sorry, Zetta?"

"So sorry," Zetta muttered. For every single decision she'd made since leaving town to go to her aunt's house.

"See, Dragon?" Ashton asked. "Please let her on."

The dragon huffed again, refusing to let Zetta climb up. But Zetta wasn't about to let a dragon with a grudge ruin her day. She could outsmart its little lizard brain. Now that she had the blaze powder she'd dumped out of her brewing stand, she could make more potions. "I'll be right back," she said. She ran into her aunt's brewing room, and got to work on an invisibility potion.

But as soon as she began pulling the ingredients from her pack, something dawned on her. She also had what she needed to make a healing potion. She took the melon slice Rift had given her and the gold from her mining first rights, and crafted a glistering melon.

Zetta paid close attention to everything she was doing, and in no time, she held the finished concoctions before her. She drank one of the invisibility potions. Almost immediately, she felt the magic consume her. Her fingers disappeared first, then her hands, arms, shoulders. Body, legs. All she could make out of herself were the tiny particles of magic that drifted off from her skin . . .

And her boots. Oops. She didn't want to leave behind her only armor, but she definitely didn't want to risk spooking the dragon, so she stored them away in her pack.

Now, it was like she'd completely vanished, except for the particles that were so faint you wouldn't notice them unless you knew right where to look. Satisfied and a little proud, Zetta put the other potions in her pack and then ran back outside and whispered to Ashton, "I'm ready."

"Where are you?" he asked, looking around.

"I made an invisibility potion. Am I . . . totally gone?"

"I don't see you. Not a bit of you. Good job!"

Zetta perked at the encouragement. This time, Ashton distracted the dragon with hard pats while Zetta jumped up right behind him. The dragon seemed a little ill-at-ease, but didn't buck or flinch when she got on. Success!

Then all she had to do was hold on for dear life as those giant wings started flapping again. All the animals in the pens bucked and complained, but soon Zetta and Ashton and the dragon were off, and Aunt Meryl's home started getting smaller and smaller. In no time they were back at their hideout in the woods.

"Easy as pumpkin pie," Ashton said. The dragon purred, then plopped onto its back for belly scritches. Ashton complied, now having to crawl up on the dragon's stomach to do so. Next thing Zetta knew, the two were play-wrestling. Zetta flinched as the dragon's giant paw pinned Ashton to the ground. The dragon was gentle, but those claws were way too sharp.

"Rift and Rayne should be back soon," Zetta said. "Maybe we need to calm the dragon down some."

"Not yet," Ashton said as the dragon let him up. He pulled Meechie the shovel out of his pack and held it in front of the dragon. "Just one more game of tug." Ashton held the stick side of the shovel and pointed the face to the dragon. The dragon's maw slipped over it, gently, but Zetta couldn't help but wince at how close those teeth were to Ashton's fingers as they tugged back and forth.

"I think maybe the dragon has outgrown Meechie. It might as well be a toothpick now. It's bound to break, and I don't want to be anywhere nearby when that happens." That dragon loved Meechie with a passion.

"We'll be fine," Ashton said, a new cockiness to his voice that Zetta wasn't familiar with.

He flies one mythical dragon, Zetta thought, *and all of a sudden, he's got a big head.*

"You shouldn't worry so much," Ashton continued. "Besides,

it's a well-documented fact that rough play is a great way to practice fighting skills. Ocelots do it. Foxes do it. Why not dragons?"

Zetta shook her head. "What kind of skills?" she asked.

"Fighting skills. It's a dragon. Sooner or later, it's going to be all on its own and it'll need to protect itself."

Zetta nodded. Ashton could teach it to protect itself . . . or he could teach it to protect their town. She realized that when she'd assessed their team's skills, she'd forgotten to include someone. Ashton was great with the dragon, and could train it to do just about anything.

"Hey, Ashton," Zetta said in a voice as sweet as sugar sucked right from the cane. "Instead of teaching the dragon to be less destructive . . . do you think you can teach it to be *more* destructive?"

Zetta couldn't believe the words that were coming out of her mouth as she watched Ashton and the dragon wrestle over Meechie, each taking turns being the aggressor.

"What?" Ashton asked as he gave a huge tug that dislodged the soggy, saliva-covered shovel from the dragon's mouth.

"Nothing," Zetta said quickly. That was a bad idea. A very bad idea. The dragon wasn't a weapon for them to use against illagers. And it wasn't a pet. It was just a mistake she'd made.

A really, really bad mistake.

CHAPTER
FOURTEEN

Zetta had a hard time shaking her idea of using the dragon against the illagers. It was pretty much all she'd thought about during her mining training session yesterday evening. The awful idea had also kept her up all night, and now it was all she could think about on the run to the mountain this morning. She was so overworked and tired and distracted that she ran straight into a cactus. Having a faceful of spines wasn't the best way to start the day, but she was fully alert now, and the sting was mostly gone by the time she and Ashton reached their hideout in the forest clearing.

Maybe it wasn't an awful idea to use the dragon as a weapon. It was big, strong, and intimidating. The illagers would probably get scared just seeing it and turn around without a single arrow being fired. Zetta decided to talk to everyone about it before the twins left, but she didn't get a chance to utter a single word. As soon as they arrived, Rift was pushing her over to a new contraption that he'd built while she was away.

"Finally," Rift said. "What took y'all so long?"

"Zetta overslept," Ashton tattled.

Zetta shot her cousin a stern look. He grinned, then ran off to wrestle with the dragon.

"Sorry," Zetta mumbled to Rift. "All this back-and-forth has me worn out. But I've got this great idea—"

"Oh, you look tired," Rift said, interrupting her. "Why don't you have a seat and rest up a bit first." He pointed at a little seat on his new contraption. It was made of slime blocks and pistons and another block Zetta had never seen. It was black, with a little gray face on one side and a blinking red light in the back. Even exhausted and sleep-deprived, Zetta could tell this was a trap.

"Not gonna happen," she said, looking at the contraption. "What's it going to do, catapult me up the mountain?"

"Something like that." Rift sighed. "Was I that obvious?"

"You were salivating like a hungry wolf staring at a skeleton bone," Zetta said. "What does it do?"

"I got it from your mom's notebook. It's an elevator. You see, the pistons and observers—" As soon as Rift started explaining the technical aspects of his contraptions, Zetta's mind started to wander. Was this how Rift felt when she was talking to him about potions?

She glanced over at Ashton, who was waving Meechie in front of the dragon's nose. The dragon snapped at it, but Ashton pulled it away. The sound of those sharp white teeth clacking together sent a chill down Zetta's spine. Ashton continued to tease the dragon, running circles around it. At first it was all in good fun, but then the dragon's usually chipper demeanor seemed to shift suddenly.

"Okay, that's enough," Zetta said. "Be nice."

Ashton grinned. "All right, Dragon. You ready? You ready? Go get it!" Ashton fake-tossed the shovel into the woods and the dragon sprung after it, sniffing and sniffing around.

Zetta shook her head, remembering when she'd done a similar thing. "You really shouldn't tease the dragon," Zetta warned, but the dragon was already bounding back toward Ashton.

The playfulness was completely gone now. The dragon was mad.

"Throw Meechie," Zetta said, but before Ashton had a chance, the dragon landed right next to him, nostrils flaring.

"I'm sorry, Dragon, I—"

The dragon huffed, but this time a purple cloud slipped from its nostrils. The cloud lingered near the ground, drifting toward Ashton like a slow-rolling fog. Ashton tried to run, but he was surrounded. He screamed as the fog overwhelmed him. A scream like Zetta had never heard. The kid was in serious pain.

The scream also broke the dragon from its anger, and those dangerous eyes puffed back into those of a concerned pup. It sniffed at the poison, like it was unsure of what it was or if it had even caused it. The dragon huffed again, the hard breath from its nostrils dissipating the purple cloud. Then it whimpered, watching as Ashton squirmed on the ground, struggling to breathe.

Zetta ran over, trying to rouse Ashton. But it was useless.

"What's going on?" Rayne said, suddenly at her side. Rift quickly fetched a bucket of water from the nearby stream.

"The dragon, I think it poisoned—" Then she remembered the healing potion she'd made and pulled it out of her pack. She put it close to Ashton's lips and made him drink. The liquid drained down his throat. It smelled sweet and syrupy, with medicinal undertones. Ashton choked on it at first, and Zetta was afraid he'd spit it back up, but the whole bottle went down smoothly after that.

Ashton stopped writhing and began to look more at peace as the potion worked its magic. Rift dabbed a damp cloth against his forehead. Soon he seemed much better.

"We have to tell someone," Rayne said. "This has gotten too big for us to handle."

"Agreed," Zetta said, even though she knew she was going to get into some serious trouble for breaking the egg in the first place. But the dragon had almost killed Ashton, and even if it might seem to be on its best behavior now, she wasn't willing to risk that it wouldn't happen again.

"It isn't the dragon's fault," Ashton said. "I shouldn't have teased it. Please, give Dragon another chance?"

Zetta bit her lip. She couldn't believe she'd actually considered using the dragon as a weapon. The reality was that it was as hostile as hostile mobs came, and they had no real control over it.

"The dragon did seem really sorry," Rift said, not helping, as always.

"Imagine what the dragon could learn in another week," Ashton said, his eyes pleading and his lips pouting. "Please?"

Zetta turned away from him. She knew she couldn't resist that face. "It's too dangerous," she said sternly. "Ashton, why don't you go play over there. *Away* from the dragon. The twins and I need to talk."

Ashton sulked off, sat down next to the campfire, and pulled out his notebook.

"Okay, what are we going to do?" said Zetta.

"We've got to tell the mayor," Rayne said.

"And what is she going to do with a three-ton beast?" Rift asked. "I think the dragon deserves another chance. I mean, that poison . . . Imagine if we taught the dragon how to use it on illagers . . ."

Zetta shook her head. "The dragon isn't a weapon," she spat out like she hadn't had the same exact idea. But seeing Ashton hurting like that, almost losing him, had changed her. "We've got my mother's notebook. We've got our brains. That'll be enough. I'm sorry, Rift, but the dragon has to—"

"Ahhhhh!" came Ashton's screams. Zetta sprung to her feet, scared that the dragon had poisoned him again, but instead, Ashton was caught on one of the pistons of Rift's new contraption. "Help me. I'm stuck."

But before Rift could come to his rescue, Ashton kicked the lever on the machine, and the contraption started gyrating and clicking and rising into the air. Ashton was dragged along with it. He managed to climb up onto one of the blocks and unstick himself, but now he was high up enough that a jump would cause considerable damage.

"Water!" Rift yelled, dumping the water bucket on the ground. "It'll break his fall."

Zetta looked down at the small, barely-there puddle with a skeptical brow. "Was this part of your prank, too? This is too dangerous, Rift. What were you thinking?" She was yelling at her friend. She didn't mean to, but this was life or death.

"Just jump!" Rift called up to Ashton. "It's safe."

"I'm too scared," Ashton said, his voice sounding more and more distant.

Zetta looked over at the dragon. It was cowering, head tucked under a bush, the rest of it clearly visible. "Dragon!" she said, no-nonsense. The dragon turned its head to her.

"You are going to fly me up there so I can save Ashton. I'm not taking no for an answer." The dragon seemed to get the gist of what she was saying, and Zetta climbed up onto its back. She didn't have time to be scared this time. The dragon's wings flapped and its weight shifted, and then the world dropped from under her. She was flying. She held on as the dragon drove straight up toward the clouds.

It wasn't long before she heard Ashton's screaming. Then she saw him, clinging to the slime block contraption for dear life. The dragon swooped, dipped, then rose, matching Ashton's ascent. The dragon eased up some, until Ashton hopped onto its back with little more than an "Oof."

The poor kid still looked terrified, though. He went limp and passed out. The dragon set Ashton and Zetta back down, safe and sound. Rift looked on in amazement. Rayne took a few timid steps toward the dragon, closer than they'd ever dared to get to the beast.

"You did good," Rayne muttered, patting the dragon on the snout.

The dragon had broken everyone's trust, but with that brave maneuver, it was hard not to forgive it. Still, they could never forget the power it held. And the hidden dangers.

CHAPTER
FIFTEEN

"Oh, all right," Zetta said. "We'll put the dragon on proba-
tion. But one more incident and it's gone for good, got it?"

Ashton ran over to the sulking dragon and rustled its ears. "Did
you hear that, Dragon? You're staying with us!" The dragon
perked, cocking its head to one side like it was trying to figure out
what Ashton was saying. Then it licked Ashton's face, its tongue
more like a small, moist blanket. Ashton smiled through the glaze
of saliva. "We're going to have to teach you not to do that," he
said.

Zetta laughed to herself. Deep inside, she was glad their little
team was staying intact. "One thing, though," she said. "I think
we should move the dragon closer to town. This running back
and forth has been draining on all of us."

Everyone agreed. Zetta would still have to come back to check
on her aunt's place, but she could leave the animals enough water

and food for a few days and they'd be fine. Then Zetta could shift her focus to making poison potions for the arrow tips.

The twins started disassembling Rift's contraption, opting to run back to town instead of riding on the dragon. They extinguished the campfire, packed up their crafting table and furnaces, and tore down the little wooden shack. Zetta planned to reuse the wood to craft arrows. She knew they'd agreed not to bring resources back with them, but it would take months to scour the desert for enough dead bushes to supply her with all the sticks she'd need. After an hour, their little clearing looked almost exactly how they'd found it.

The dragon didn't balk at Zetta's presence on its back this time. They took off once more, and soon the mountain started getting farther and farther away, until it was just a bump on the horizon. The welcome sight of sand below them calmed Zetta. She watched as Ashton leaned this way and that, the dragon turning slightly at each movement. They truly had an amazing bond. Ashton leaned forward and the dragon started to dip. The ground crept up on them gradually, the town still so far off in the distance that no one would spot a giant flying mob in the sky, but not so far that they couldn't get back and forth by foot in less than thirty minutes.

Without potions.

Ashton angled them once more to a cave set into a large hill. Perfect spot to keep a dragon hidden. As the pads of the dragon's paws kissed the earth, a flood of relief filled Zetta from head to toe. They'd made it with no problems.

Zetta leaned against a rock and rested while Ashton and the dragon played hide-and-seek. Ashton would hide behind a cactus or over a hill or in a cave, and then the dragon would sniff him out. It was pretty cute. Then they'd wrestle, roughhousing like one of them hadn't nearly killed the other just over an hour ago.

Zetta sighed. It was an accident. A once-in-a-lifetime accident.

She placed their crafting table down in a handy spot, converted the cabin logs into wood planks, and then started whittling the planks into sticks for the arrows. How many would they even need? Hundreds? Thousands?

"Whatcha doing?" Ashton asked, trotting up to Zetta with the dragon on his heels. The dragon was seriously interested in the sticks. The pile was growing, and Zetta's hands were already starting to go numb.

"Making arrows."

"Cool! Nana and Papa are gonna be prepping a bunch of chickens for the Eve of Hostile Mobs festival. I'll have a ton of feathers for you." He reached into his pack. "Here are a couple to get you started."

"Really?" Zetta asked. "That'd be great." She smiled, glad the townspeople were still celebrating in spite of all the hardships they'd had since the attack. "I suppose you're too old for masks this year?" she asked.

"Yeah, probably. But Rift and Rayne said I could help out on their float!"

Zetta grinned a tight grin. She'd helped Rift and Rayne with their family float one year, and never again. Their parents were just so intense. Every little detail had to be perfect. They'd made a giant cave spider that year, and put redstone torches in the eyes so they lit up and everything. They had a creepy taxidermy spider that served as their reference. They'd scaled it up so that it took five people to operate it, one for each pair of legs and one for the head, turning it this way and that, and opening and closing the fang-filled mouth. They'd gotten second place that year, and Zetta went a whole six months hearing about how they'd been robbed and should have gotten the first-place trophy and all the bragging rights that came with it.

Phew. "Yeah, good luck with that," Zetta mumbled. "Well, we'll still need flint, so I guess I'll work on that next. Why don't you head back? I might be late tonight."

Ashton gave the dragon a final nuzzle, then took off.

There was still so much for Zetta to do. She took out her stone pickaxe and explored the caves until she found some gravel to mine, gaining a few pieces of flint from them in the process. Slowly, it was all starting to come together. After crafting some arrows, she pulled a healing potion from her pack.

How did making tipped arrows work? Zetta tried dipping the arrowhead into the potion. Nothing. She tried all kinds of combinations on the crafting table, but she could not make the arrows magic.

"I think I'm missing an ingredient," she said to the dragon, curled up next to her.

The dragon looked at her and huffed. Little flecks of purple poison flared out of its nostrils. Not enough to reach her, but enough to make her nervous. "Stop that. We told you— keep your dragon breath to yourself!"

Then it hit Zetta. Hadn't her aunt said something about dragon's breath and potioning? She ran over to the little cloud and carefully collected some in every bottle she had on her. She was ready to experiment further, but she needed to get back home so she could sleep a bit and then do her mining training, like she was a noob.

Despite being sleepy, Zetta tried her hardest in mining class, listening as Milo taught people who were still struggling to figure out the correct way to hold a pickaxe. It was basic-level instruction, but she still learned a few things, and when Milo let them go practice, Zetta ended up discovering two iron veins. She called first rights, scoring herself two more iron ores. Now she had enough for an iron pickaxe. Even Milo was impressed.

After class, Zetta wanted so badly to slip into her bed, but those arrows weren't going to make themselves. She hurried home, and snuck her brewing stand out of the closet. It still had a tiny bit of blaze powder in it, and after a few tries, Zetta had herself a lingering potion. She packed the stand away where her father had hidden it, hoping he wouldn't notice she'd been back in there. Then she took off to share the good news with her friends.

She arrived at the cave on the outskirts of town in no time. Rift had set up an arrow contraption using instructions from Zetta's mother's notebook. Rayne was training the dragon to dive-bomb armor stands with its snout. It did so with remarkable accuracy. Zetta loved the sound of those giant flapping wings so much. Armor stand after armor stand went flying off, landing in broken pieces. Rayne patted the dragon lovingly on the snout, then gathered the armor stand pieces, recrafted them, and started the process all over.

"Um, you're not teaching the dragon to fight, are you?" she said to Rayne. "I thought we talked about that."

"I know, I know," Rayne said as the dragon nudged them, trying to get Rayne to hurry up with setting the stands up again. Rayne gave the dragon a hip bump, and the dragon retaliated by licking the side of Rayne's face. "But look how accurate Dragon is. Didn't you see how easily it took those targets out? I think we should at least consider it."

Zetta grumbled to herself, though she had to admit, Rayne and the dragon were pretty cute together.

"I've got a few arrows for you," Zetta said, handing a dozen regular arrows over to Rift.

"Awesome," he said, but he spoke like his mind was far off in diagrams and calculations. "Where's Ashton?"

"Helping our grandparents with festival stuff. You need any help with anything?" she asked.

"Actually, if you could press this button when I say, that'd be handy." Rift walked around to the other side of the machine and examined the piles of red dust snaking from block to block. "Okay . . . now."

Zetta pressed the button. She watched as the dull red dust lit up bright. There were all sorts of doodads spaced between the dust trails.

Rift yelled "Aha!" and pointed to the spot where the dust stopped lighting up. "Found the problem. Thanks." He tinkered a bit more, then loaded the arrows into a chest mounted up top. "Ready for a test?"

Zetta nodded.

"Hey, Rayne. Line those targets up like we talked about?" Rift asked as he walked around his arrow-flinging contraption one more time.

Rayne moved the armor stands thirty feet from the contraption, then quickly got out of the way.

"Firing in three. Two. One." Rift pressed the button, and a little glowstone lamp lit up, but nothing else happened.

"Um—" Zetta started.

"Wait for it," Rift said, raising a finger to silence her. Then a storm of arrows shot out in rapid succession. Pftt. Pftt. Pftt. Cutting through the air and sinking into the targets. It lasted only seconds, but when the dust settled, every single armor stand was teeming with arrows. No illager could survive that much of an onslaught.

"That was amazing!" Zetta said, jumping up and down.

"Get me about ten times as many arrows, and we might not even need the dragon to defend our town."

"We're not using the dragon to defend our town," Zetta repeated. She was starting to sound like a broken music disc.

"What's the status on the poison-tipped arrows?" Rayne asked.

"I'm super-close. Maybe today."

Rayne nodded, trying to read her. "It's just that you promised us poison-tipped arrows, and—"

"I'll get them to you soon, okay?" Ugh. "Anyway, why don't you and Rift head home. I'm sure your parents are wanting to practice for the festival parade or something."

"You're sure you can handle the dragon yourself?" Rayne asked. "I can stay if—"

"Yeah, no, it's fine. I can handle it." She could use a little alone time after the day she'd had in the mines, all huddled up with nine other miners who could barely swing a pickaxe. She'd nearly taken a shot in the forehead.

She loaded the shovel thrower and watched as the dragon ran back and forth, chasing Meechie and then dropping it into the dropper, only for it to shoot out again. And again. And again.

The contraption firing was a soothing rhythm. Zetta didn't even notice it lulling her to sleep.

But when she woke, she definitely noticed that the rhythm had stopped, and that the dragon was nowhere to be seen.

CHAPTER
SIXTEEN

Zetta jumped to her feet and started searching frantically for the dragon, checking all the nearby caves. Checking over each sand dune, even checking in the places she logically knew a dragon couldn't fit. But there was no sign of it, and worse, there weren't any tracks to go by. The dragon had flown off this time.

Maybe another molting? So soon? Argh. How could she be so careless?

She had to get the others to help. Ashton would be so furious with her. She didn't want to face him, but if they had a chance of finding the dragon before the situation got too heated, she needed him. She ran as fast as she could to her grandparents' farm. She was heading to the house, but heard a strange cooing coming from the barn, the same noises Ashton would make when fussing over the chickens. Zetta zagged that way instead, but when she pulled the door latch it was locked. It was never locked.

She heard laughter and gruff noises coming from inside, so she knocked. The laughter stopped, and then she heard shushing.

"Who is it?" came her cousin's voice.

"Zetta. Do you have company? I've got . . . news."

The lock clicked and the latch opened. When the door slid open, she saw her cousin's blank face staring back at her. "I think I know what your news is," he grumbled, then pulled her in and shut the door again.

The chickens all looked panicked and had flown up to the rafters. When Zetta saw a long black tail peeking out from behind a huge stack of hay bales, she understood why.

The dragon had come here.

"Care to explain why there's a dragon in my barn, cousin?" Ashton asked.

Zetta fumbled for words. "I—uh. . . . must have dozed off for a bit. But I've been doing mining training, and prepping arrows, and watching the dragon. It's just too much."

"It's fine," Ashton said. He must have felt sorry for her, because his accusatory demeanor disappeared and was replaced with one of understanding. "We're all in this together. Good thing we practiced all that tracking, or who knows where the dragon would have ended up."

"Did anyone see it?" Zetta asked.

"Papa almost did. We were out in the far fields when I saw a black dot flying at us. I told him the hoes really needed sharpening, so he went off to do that before the dragon arrived. I got it into the barn as fast as I could. But it was close, Zetta. Too close. We have to be more careful."

Zetta nodded. "I've got a couple more invisibility potions on me. If we can get the dragon to drink one, then we can get it back to the cave without worrying over it being seen."

Ashton shrugged. "We could. But wouldn't it be better to keep the dragon closer? We're all worn out. Even running back and forth to the caves is a lot."

"You're not suggesting that we keep the dragon here, are you? How are we supposed to keep that thing hidden? It's not going to be happy cooped up in this barn all day and night."

Ashton smiled, then picked up a piece of paper from the floor and folded it carefully until it resembled a flower. Then he stuck it on the dragon's snout. The dragon snuffed, but then seemed to forget about it when Ashton started scratching behind its horn. Zetta spent a long moment confused, but then it dawned on her. The Eve of Hostile Mobs festival was just a few days off. It was the time of year when giant paper flower floats designed to look like hostile mobs were celebrated by the whole town as they were carried through the streets.

"You want to turn the dragon into a float . . ." Zetta said, skeptical.

"Why not? It's perfect. We're going to have to tell the town about the dragon eventually anyway. Why not after it's won first place in the festival parade? We can show how much control we have over it, show off all the tricks it knows, too. The mayor will instantly see how useful it'll be during a raid."

Zetta shook her head. A sickly chill churned in her stomach. Not this again.

"We have to decide if we trust this dragon enough to protect us or not," Ashton said with a serious face.

Zetta knew this. Maybe that's what she was most afraid of. Trusting that something good would come from her biggest mistake. Maybe it was like how two wrongs make a right? Wait, that wasn't how the saying went. But maybe a big wrong and a big right would cancel each other out somehow. She imagined how great it would feel to come clean to everyone.

"Okay," Zetta said. "I still think it's risky, but you're right. If we're going to trust the dragon, we need to trust it. And I trust you . . . so. Let's do it."

Ashton pumped his fist in the air and screamed, riling up the few chickens that lingered nearby. "Sorry, Salma! Pardon, Nella," he said, giving their wattles a tickle. They loved back on him, rubbing their heads against his hand.

"Anyway, this will give me a good excuse to get out of working on the float with Rift and Rayne and their parents."

"A lot already?" Zetta said, trying to muffle her laugh.

"Do you know how many spikes an elder guardian has?" Ashton asked.

Zetta shook her head.

"Twelve. And they have to be spaced apart just right. And be the exact same size down to a fourth of an inch. And extend and retract all together at the exact same time. And if you're responsible for extending spikes four, five, six, and seven, and are a second and a half late, then you get a lecture about that time their family float could have gotten first place if one of the spider eyes hadn't lost its redstone torch halfway through the parade." Ashton took a deep breath, then sighed. "Sorry. Still a little jittery."

"No, I get it. So we're going rogue with our own float. Sweet."

"I figure we can put some flowers here and there, just to make the dragon look a little more decorative. Then if anyone asks what we're doing holed up in the barn all the time, we can say we're just preparing our float. No big deal."

Zetta groaned. It wasn't exactly a lie, but she wasn't excited that her half-truths were rubbing off on her cousin.

Zetta felt like she was carrying the entire Overworld's fate in her hands. She headed out to the farm and slashed down as much sugarcane as she could carry. When she was back in the barn, she crafted it into paper. Then Ashton dusted the paper with purple concrete powder, a long-standing tradition that the town of Sienna Dunes only observed during the festival. The vibrant purple paper would look great against the dragon's black scales. Then they folded flowers well into the night, until a knock came at the barn door.

"Who is it?" said Ashton and Zetta in unison.

"Zetta? What's going on? Why aren't you at the caves?" came Rayne's voice.

"And where's the you-know-what?" Rift added.

Zetta had been so caught up in folding flowers that she totally forgot she needed to tell them that they'd moved their operations to the barn. She hopped up and ran over to the door and unfastened the lock. She peeked outside to make sure no one was watching, then ushered her friends inside. They took one look at the flower-covered dragon, then looked at each other.

"No," Rayne said. "I can't do this."

"Ashton and I already had this conversation," Zetta said. "You were right. The dragon could help us defend the town. We've worked closely with it and we can trust it. And we can show off that trust by having the dragon perform at the festival parade."

"I mean, yeah, I get that. But I literally can't do this. If I have to fold another flower, I'm going to be sick."

"Well, I think it looks great," said Rift. "There's only one problem."

"What's that?" Ashton asked, concern on his face.

"You're totally going to get first place, and then Rayne and I are going to have to spend the rest of the year hearing about how our parents were robbed of victory *again*. But it'll be worth it. The town needs to see how much work we've put into the dragon. They'll be thanking us soon enough."

"You all right, Rayne?" Zetta asked her friend, who was looking legitimately queasy.

"Yeah," they said, backing up toward the door. "I'm just going to go get some fresh air. For a minute. Or several."

Then Rayne was gone.

Rift sighed, annoyed and maybe a little embarrassed by his twin, but Zetta understood. Festival time could be intense for everyone; the holidays could be draining. In a close-knit community like Sienna Dunes, there was always someone underfoot, always a cousin or friend or aunty or uncle in need of help, or someone looking to spread some gossip along with their holiday cheer.

It could be a lot. It made Zetta miss her aunt even more, now that she knew exactly who she was missing. Zetta hoped her father would want to see his sister too someday. They'd drawn a line in the sand a long time ago, and both of them were too stubborn to cross it right now, but maybe that wouldn't always be the case.

"Rayne will help out when they're ready," Zetta said. She hoped Rift and Rayne would never drift apart like her father and aunt had.

"Question," Rift said, examining the flower-covered dragon from all angles. "The floats are normally made of paper and bamboo scaffolding . . . light enough for a few people to carry. How do you expect to carry this dragon through the streets? It must weigh a few tons."

Ashton perked up. "I'm glad you asked! I plan to use some leads and sticks tied to the legs and wings to make it look like we're doing the work of operating it." Ashton demonstrated, calling the dragon to heel by his side. He stretched a lead around the dragon's ankle, then tied the other end to a bamboo stick. He gently tugged up and the dragon responded by lifting its leg. "We've been practicing a bit," Ashton explained. "But Zetta and I will need at least two more people to help operate the float." He looked pleadingly at Rift.

Rift shook his head. "I can't. It's one thing if my parents lose to you. It's a whole 'nother thing to lose to their own kids."

"There's no one else we can trust with the dragon," Ashton

pleaded. "It already knows you. It trusts you. Besides, this isn't about winning. It's about saving our town."

"I can't believe I'm actually considering this," Rift said, exasperated. He took the stick and lead from Ashton, then gave a little tug. The dragon responded in the same manner as it had with Ashton. "Okay, I'll do it. But I get to work a wing."

Ashton smiled. "Awesome. Now we just need to convince Rayne."

Zetta knew how sensitive a matter this would be, so she went off alone and found Rayne setting old flowerpots on top of fence posts, then shooting them off with arrows. The accuracy of their shot was astounding, even with their frayed nerves. Zetta stood back a ways, out of their line of sight, but close enough that Rayne had to know she was there.

Zetta watched shot after shot land. Then Rayne left to collect the arrows to shoot again.

"Still waiting on those poison-tipped arrows," they said to Zetta.

Her shoulders slumped. Zetta knew she was close to making tipped arrows. Zetta also knew that Rayne was bringing up the arrows to avoid talking about what was really on their mind. "You okay?" she asked.

Rayne nodded. "Yeah."

"You can talk to me. We've been friends for forever. I'm sorry the flowers freaked you out."

"It wasn't that . . ."

"Is it your parents? I know working with them can be intense,"

Zetta offered. "I can try to talk to them. Maybe it would be different if it came from me."

"No, they're fine. I mean, yeah, they're totally obsessed with the float, just like every other year—but that's just it. They're acting like this is any other year. Nobody is talking about the raid anymore. It's almost like it never even happened. People are going on with their lives, planning for this festival, when at any moment those illagers could come back and destroy everything we love. And all my parents are worried about is getting the proportions of a giant paper elder guardian exactly right."

"Yeah, I get that," Zetta said. "I've been so busy with the dragon and mining and potioning that I haven't had a chance to really slow down and think about it either."

"I wish we could go back to how it was before. When our only concerns were running into the odd creeper while we were out on our adventures." Rayne twanged the string of their bow absentmindedly, then added, "It was easier to be the brave one back then."

Zetta laid a hand on Rayne's shoulder. "It's okay to be afraid. The world has changed in scary ways. But fears can be conquered. You remember how scared you were of Dragon at first?"

"Vaguely," Rayne teased. "Spending several hours up in a tree does change your perspective. Dragon doesn't seem so big and scary anymore. Well . . . you know what I mean."

Zetta nodded. It was easy to forget how massive and threatening the dragon was when it was constantly begging for belly scritches. "Exactly. And you don't always have to be the brave one. We've all got one another's backs. If we work together, we can make this town safe. Especially with Dragon on our side."

"I hope it's enough," Rayne said with a sigh. "But I guess your dragon float idea isn't a bad one."

"Thanks, but it was Ashton's idea really."

"Because he's always looking for ways to impress you. You're a great cousin."

Zetta felt the heat rising in her cheeks. She tried to set a good example for Ashton. She knew what it was like to grow up looking for role models. Looking for someone to be like. She was glad she could be that for Ashton.

"So I've got good news and bad news," Zetta said to Rayne. "What do you want first?"

"Bad news?"

"Bad news is that we need one more person to operate the dragon float. And it has to be you." Zetta smiled. "You can say no, of course, but then we won't be able to be in the parade and we won't get a chance to show off all our good work."

Rayne grunted. "I'm almost afraid to ask, but what's the good news? Do you have a potion that'll magically make my parents forgive me for bailing on the float they've been working on for months?"

Zetta laughed. "I make potions, not miracles. The good news is that we've got destiny by the tail, and if we pull this off, our names will go down in Sienna Dunes history."

CHAPTER
SEVENTEEN

Celebration was in the air, and the smell of fresh-cut fruit and roasting meat and boiling stews was making Zetta want to crawl out of her skin. This wasn't the day to skip breakfast, but her nerves were tight, and her mind was focused on the dragon's performance. So she blocked out the distractions and took her place next to it. The dragon was more purple paper flowers than scales now, but it looked magnificent. It even seemed proud to be dressed up in such finery.

They'd practiced as much as they could, perfecting their routine. Zetta knew it so well, she had dreams about it. More like nightmares, she had to admit. She was in charge of the left back leg and the ridiculously long tail, and in her dreams, the dragon would get overexcited and start swinging its tail, knocking over vendor carts packed on either side of the street, crashing through storefront windows, and sometimes colliding with people, sending them flying clear to the other side of town.

Zetta tightened her grip on the bamboo pole—the one with the lead tied to the dragon's tail—knowing good and well that one halfhearted yank by the dragon would rip it right out of her hands.

"Don't be nervous," Ashton said to her, peeking under the dragon's belly. Did the uneasiness show that much on her face? "You get nervous, Dragon gets nervous."

Zetta nodded and swallowed her fears. She heard cheering in the distance for the floats that had gone before. The dragon float was at the very end of the line since it was a last-minute addition to the parade. Finally, the two floats in front of them started to move. There was the giant ghast two floats ahead. Zetta could only see the back of it, but it was impressive. She could hardly believe that somewhere in the nether right now, Aunt Meryl was fighting the real thing.

Four operators stood below the paper version of the ghast, dressed in all-black outfits, looking like shadows as the long bamboo poles they held twisted and turned, high up in the sky. The ghast turned in kind, and the audience lined up on either side of the street screamed and laughed when the ghast spat out giant wads of orange and red paper, imitating fireballs. Some of the younger kids cried until they figured out what was going on. Zetta smiled, remembering fondly how terrified she'd been her first festival, and how she'd grown to love that little bit of fear once a year.

Rayne muttered something.

"You okay over there?" Zetta asked, the smile falling off her face. Things were different now. That once-a-year safe sort of fear had been replaced with something else. Rayne had to be feeling that, too.

"Yeah," Rayne said. "Let's just get this over with."

The float directly in front of the dragon started about a minute later, a wither skeleton. Zetta could make out a music player mounted inside its rib cage, filling the street with the sound of bones rattling. The people of Sienna Dunes appreciated little touches like that. One of the operators swung the skeleton's sword in front of it, coming so close to the crowd that the people in the front row had to jump back.

Some years things did get a little dangerous, but those who chose to watch the parade from close up got bragging rights for the rest of the year. Since the paper flower props were so light, usually the bruises they received were minor. But if this dragon decided to—

Zetta stopped her train of thought. Everything would be fine. The dragon would perform perfectly.

Finally, it was Zetta and her friends' turn to go. Zetta put on her best smile and started forward, clutching the bamboo sticks close and raising and lowering the leg pole as the dragon stepped, while simultaneously swinging the pole for the tail back and forth. Pretending to operate the dragon took a lot more effort than she'd initially thought. Coordination was everything.

The oohs and aahs came almost instantly. There were several kids in the crowd who had dressed up like ender dragons as well, and they seemed particularly excited. The dragon float was a spectacle, even for the most spectacular festival of Sienna Dunes.

Ashton led the way up front, turning the dragon's head left and right, up and down. Or at least that's what he appeared to be doing. In reality, the dragon was doing all the work, watching Ashton for cues. It kept heeling perfectly.

"Whoa!" Rift said from in front of Zetta. She looked up and saw that his grip on the wing pole had come loose. Now the dragon appeared to be flapping on its own, so hard that the wings started generating lift and the dragon's front paws came off the ground.

The crowd's cheering intensified, however. Rift jumped up and grabbed the pole and Ashton whispered a command to the dragon for it to calm down. Chanting began soon after: *Ender Dragon! Ender Dragon! Ender Dragon!*

The crowd favorite was already chosen. But the award for best float would be decided by Mayor Maxine. At last, they reached the town square, all sixteen floats taking their spots around the grand stairway of the town hall, which had been set up to serve as a stage. A lectern had been converted into a podium, and potted cacti were arranged on either side as decoration. In front of the lectern sat a single, random sandstone block.

"Zetta! Zetta!" came her father's voice.

Once the dragon was settled and in its place, Zetta turned around, and smiled as she saw her father running through the crowd to get to her. "That was amazing," he said, nearly out of breath. "Why didn't you tell me this was what you were being so secretive about?"

Zetta shrugged. "You know, I guess I just wanted it to be a surprise."

Her father beamed. "I get that, but I was really worried. I really thought you were keeping something important from me . . . I'm glad to know this was all it was. Amazing job."

Zetta nodded. Tears punched at the corners of her eyes, but she somehow kept them from breaking through. There was more she was hiding from him. So much more, but it would all come out soon enough.

The mayor stood on the stage, beaming at Zetta as well. Zetta didn't think she'd ever seen Mayor Maxine look at her with anything other than a scowl. Maybe a stern grimace. "I think the winner of this year's festival will come as a surprise to no one," the mayor said. "But first, we must talk about why this festival is so important in this time of uncertainty. It was hard for some of us to find reason to celebrate in the face of adversity and fear. Some even called for us to cancel the celebration this year. But adversity is exactly the reason we needed to continue this long-standing tradition. Illagers may come. They may smash our buildings, take our valuables. But they will never smash our spirit."

Applause erupted from the crowd. Zetta looked over and saw that Rayne was clapping too. Maybe those were the exact words they needed to hear. Zetta felt the words, too. Sienna Dunes would persevere.

The mayor grabbed the sandstone block sitting on the stage and walked toward the bell tower. "It took us a week to get our town back together, with everyone chipping in, working day and night. And this stone here is the very last block that needs to be placed to make our town whole again."

Like so many of the buildings in town, the bell tower had been badly damaged in the raid, and now the mayor shoved the stone block into the only remaining gap. Warm applause filled the streets for nearly a whole minute. It was contagious. Electrifying. It was perfect.

Just like the dragon.

"And now, without further ado, the winner of this year's mob festival is the float entitled 'The Ender Dragon' operated by Ashton Night, Zetta Night, Rayne Solomon-Lee, and Rift Solomon-Lee!"

More applause. Zetta and her friends made their way up to the stage, with Ashton staying back with the dragon, just in case. Little kids in hostile mob costumes danced around him, their pudgy little hands petting the dragon all over, and Ashton didn't seem even a little bit concerned the dragon would hurt any of them. The dragon loved all the attention. More friends never hurt.

Zetta stood a few feet behind the podium at the center of the stage where she'd give her speech. She felt her stomach drop to her feet. This was it. The moment she was excited about and at the same time feared more than anything else. It was her time to tell the truth about the dragon being real and hope for the best.

She looked out into the crowd of beaming faces. Both her grandparents were there, waving excitedly. Zetta even saw Rift and Rayne's parents grinning at them, so proud. Perhaps her friends had had no reason to worry. Zetta warmly accepted the trophy from the mayor, then stepped up to the podium.

"Hi!" Her voice came out like a squeak. Zetta cleared her

throat and tried again. "Hello, Sienna Dunes. We thank you so much for your enthusiasm for our float. I know it's been a difficult time for a lot of people, but in this time of hardship, it's nice to have friends and family to lean on. I'm accepting this award on behalf of our team, but I couldn't have done it without Rift and Rayne, and especially my cousin Ashton over there."

The mayor smiled and gently pushed Zetta away. "Thank you so much for that amazing speech—"

"Wait!" Zetta said. "I'm not done. We have something very important to add."

The mayor laughed and pushed a pair of glasses onto her nose as she looked down at a piece of paper. "Don't we all! And I'd personally like to thank the sponsors of this year's Eve of Hostile Mobs festival. Benjamin's Slime Shop, providing slime cubes of exceptional quality to Sienna Dunes for over fifteen years. And let's not forget Julian's Fish and Chips, serving prime salmon and cod, cooked to perfection. If you're feeling brave, there's the Friday pufferfish special—finish the whole plate without getting sick, and you eat for free!"

Zetta tried to push her way back in front of the podium, but Mayor Maxine gave her that too-tight smile again and bumped her out of the way. "Why don't you show that shiny gold trophy off to the rest of your team," the mayor said. "And today's fruit feast was brought to you by my favorite grocer, and yours, Gloriana! Can we get a round of applause for that melon sculpture shaped like a sea turtle? What a work of art! And let's hear it for all of our magnificent vendors today."

Applause erupted again.

"Our float!" Zetta shouted, realizing her chance was drawing to a close. Soon the crowd would empty from the streets. "It's not actually a float. It's a *real* ender dragon and we want it to help protect our—"

But the audience was too loud for her words to cut through. Fireworks exploded overhead. Dozens and dozens of them. Green and lime green and white, dazzling the crowd against the evening sky. She'd forgotten about them. Usually it was the best part of the festivities, watching the display as the night set in, but when Zetta looked back at the dragon, she could see in its eyes that it was spooked.

Big-time.

Its tail swayed nervously, though all eyes were focused on the sky, so nobody noticed. Ashton tried to calm the dragon, but it wasn't working. The dragon broke away from him, gruffing and huffing and flapping its wings. Zetta, Rift, and Rayne sprinted over, each grabbing a bamboo pole and trying to pull the dragon back into submission, but this just made the dragon angrier. It tore loose of the leads. It thrashed and bit at the poles tethered to its body, destroying several of the food carts set up nearby. The overturned fruit was crushed under its giant paws, and a vat of boiling stew spilled on its tail.

The dragon yelped out and its tail slammed into the side of the just-restored bell tower, obliterating a huge section of blocks. Sandstone dust flew everywhere as the dragon scurried away from the crowd and the noise, but not before doing a massive shake that dislodged most of the paper flowers glued to its scales. The overly cute dragon float didn't look quite so cute anymore.

Screams came next, lots of them. Ashton tried to take off after the dragon, but Nana was suddenly as spry as the desert was dry, and grabbed him by the shirt collar. "I need to have a word with you, Ashton," Nana said, looking fierce.

Zetta looked back at her dad. He was running too, toward her. But she couldn't get caught. She dug in and sprinted toward the dragon, bending down to scoop up a fallen apple to munch on since hunger was starting to burn in her stomach. She didn't have any more swiftness potions, so she tried the little sprint jumping trick Ashton was always doing. It did seem to give her a little extra speed, though the world bobbing up and down like that made her dizzy. But dizziness didn't matter right now. Zetta needed to do everything she could to stop the dragon before it caused more damage.

She ran, sprinting as fast as she could, until she was in front of the dragon, staring it straight down.

"Stop!" she called to it, channeling her inner Ashton. "Halt. Heel. Stay. Sit! Stop!" The dragon kept barreling right at her, not slowing down. Zetta knew that this was no time to play chicken with a beast ten times her size, but what choice did she have at this point?

But the dragon did stop. It stared at Zetta. It breathed in and out, calm coming over its eyes. Zetta couldn't believe it. She went to grab the last remaining lead to usher the dragon to safety, but a different type of shout came from behind her. Shouts not of fear, but of bloodlust. Zetta turned around and saw several dozen townspeople, marching toward the dragon, all bearing swords.

And these swords were definitely not made from paper flowers.

CHAPTER
EIGHTEEN

"You have to get the dragon out of here!" Ashton, still caught in their grandmother's clutches, shouted at Zetta. "Now! Fly it out of here."

Fly? On a dragon? By herself? She'd done it once before. Surely she could do it again. She sidled up to the dragon, but it was having none of that and shifted away from her, purple eyes large and glassy.

"Look, I know you're scared. I'm scared, too, but if you don't let me ride you, we're both going to be in a lot of trouble." The shouts were getting closer, and those sharp swords were nearly within striking distance. She didn't think they had enough time, so she pulled out her last potion of invisibility and tried to force it into the dragon's mouth. The dragon hissed at her, and she backed off. She didn't think it would use its poison on her, but she wasn't a hundred percent sure.

"Please, please, just drink it," she pleaded. Zetta tried again, but the dragon bucked this time, wings opening wide and knocking the glass out of the grocery store window. The display was full of fresh eggs, neatly stacked in cartons of twelve. Another flap of the dragon's wings and they all went spilling into the street. Chicks hatched from some of the eggs, maybe thirty or forty of them, creating a smoke screen of feathers and squawking. The other eggs smashed into the ground, becoming a slick, yolky mess, and between these two obstacles, the vengeful townspeople came to a halt, trying to step closer but slipping and falling into each other.

Zetta noticed she was standing in front of the blacksmith's shop. It sold the best pickaxes and swords and axes, but she hadn't been able to afford anything in there the last time she'd browsed. She saw an iron shovel sitting in the display window, the glass broken out now due to the dragon's antics.

Maybe Zetta had one last trick up her sleeve. She carefully reached through the broken glass, grabbed the shovel, and then held it up to the dragon. It wasn't Meechie, but the dragon still seemed to take some interest. Zetta started running, and the dragon chased after her. She didn't stop until they were far away from town, almost all the way back to their caves. Zetta knew they couldn't stay here long. The mayor would send a search party, and they would almost certainly look here. But it was a good place to rest in the meantime.

"I'm sorry, Dragon," Zetta said. "I didn't mean to put you in such a dangerous situation. I forgot all about the fireworks. I hope you can forgive me."

The dragon was resting now, and just snorted at her. Forgiveness might be a long while coming. She'd let the dragon down twice now. Maybe it was time to admit defeat. She'd have to take the dragon back to her aunt Meryl's place, and if the dragon wasn't going to let her ride it, then it was going to be a long, long walk.

Zetta needed to get through to the dragon, and soon. How could she build up trust quickly? Maybe that was the wrong question. Trust didn't come quickly. But how could she have patience when there were people hunting the dragon this very second? Zetta slowed down, took some deep breaths. She remembered what Ashton had said about the dragon's sensing her nervousness.

She untensed her muscles, eased the frown on her face into a smile, then thought of something pleasant she could be doing instead of worrying and fretting over the next few hours of her life. If she had that much longer to live.

Zetta turned her back to the dragon and went to the shovel thrower. Meechie was still tucked safely inside, so she took it out and tossed it up and down, spinning it around like a baton. She made up a little song about it as she twirled.

> Dragon, Dragon. Friend or foe?
> Maybe we shall never know.
> Tough as bedrock, black as night
> Your eyes, they shine a purple bright.
> Please forgive me *really* soon,
> And fly us high up toward the moon.

Trust me now, it's time to go.

Dragon, Dragon. Friend or foe?

Behind her, the dragon had stopped its snorting and huffing, but Zetta didn't dare look back at it. She kept singing and twirling until she heard soft padded footsteps get closer, then stop. The dragon made a little purring sound she hadn't heard it make since it was just a pup. Still Zetta didn't acknowledge the dragon. Instead she hummed softly and slowed her twirling.

The dragon was so close now, she could feel its breath on the back of her neck. It made a louder purr, like it wanted her to throw the shovel already, but she didn't. Instead, she tossed the stick up really high in the air, and then caught it. The dragon bumped her back gently. Zetta turned around, acting like she was surprised to see the dragon there.

"Oh!" she said. "Hi, Dragon." She smiled, then turned back around and started flipping Meechie some more. The dragon came around so that they were facing each other now. It stooped into a play bow, paws out and bottom stretched up, that long tail wagging back and forth.

"So now you like me again," she said. "I'll throw it if you let me pet you." She offered the dragon the back of her hand first. It gave it a little sniff and didn't back up when she approached. She went as slowly as she could stand and petted it once on the snout, then backed up and threw the shovel. The dragon ran after it and returned it to her feet.

"Okay, good job! Now I'm going to pet you a little closer to your horns, okay?" Zetta petted the dragon twice this time, then threw the shovel again. She worked slowly, until she was petting it on the back of the neck. Then she mounted it for a couple seconds before hopping back off. Between throws of the shovel—there must have been nearly fifty in all—Zetta slowly worked her way to sitting upon the dragon for a full three minutes. When the dragon didn't seem to mind at all, she patted it.

It was getting darker, and she could see torches in the distance. They were still searching the desert for Zetta and the dragon, and they were getting closer.

"Okay, Dragon. I've been patient. But I really need you to fly for me now." Zetta leaned forward, just as Ashton had done, and gave the fly command. The dragon's wings didn't flutter, not even a little. She leaned forward again, and gave the dragon a little jostle with her heel. It huffed, and suddenly seemed aggravated to have her up there on its back.

"Sorry, sorry!" Zetta said, keeping an eye on the torches. They were moving directly toward her and the dragon now, with a sense of purpose. She must have been spotted. "Okay. Please, Dragon. Please!" She made the clicking noise that Ashton often used.

This time when Zetta leaned forward, she felt the dragon shift as well. Its massive wings came unfurled and flapped, and soon after that, the wind was slapping Zetta in the face and they were airborne. It felt amazing. The dragon took her commands like they'd been working together forever. She thought about steering them straight toward her aunt's place, but Zetta was pretty sure they'd decide to look there next. She circled around again and again, mind churning for a safe place to go while the moon shone like a beacon overhead. It was magnificent, flying like this, bonding with the dragon. She knew it would soon be over, though. Her aunt would be home from her adventure, and her time with the dragon would come to an end. Zetta was glad they hadn't given the dragon a name. It would have made it that much harder to say goodbye.

Zetta wiped what was definitely not a tear from her eye. Just the wind blowing too hard in her face. As she searched the rolling desert vista for a safe place to hide, among the sandy dunes and craggy cliffs, she spotted something—a large building, several stories high, with a large dome up top. There were lots of figures gathered nearby, milling around. Animals, too. Zetta thought it was odd. She didn't know of any other desert towns this close to theirs, and besides, it wasn't really a town, just a single building.

Curious, she guided the dragon down to get a better look, but when she saw the gray, angry faces all looking back up at her, she immediately wished she hadn't. They were illagers. Dozens and dozens of them, with several of those ravager beasts chained up, raring to go. And Zetta had a bad, bad feeling that she knew exactly where they were heading.

CHAPTER
NINETEEN

Zetta needed to get back to town and warn Mayor Maxine, but there was no way the mayor would believe her now, especially without proof. Zetta knew what she had to do. She had to get closer to this pillager outpost and grab something, anything that would prove that she'd seen what she'd seen. So she steered the dragon away from the outpost and toward a large, sandy hill and landed behind it. She tossed Meechie to the dragon to keep it busy, along with a command to stay. The dragon seemed to smile at her before it started gnawing on the end of the shovel.

Then Zetta downed an invisibility potion in three gulps and waited for the tingling sensation to kick in. She was invisible. Totally invisible. Oh, but as she looked down, she saw her boots again. Oops. She took them off and stashed them in her pack. She was completely vulnerable with no armor at all, but she didn't have a choice.

She trekked through the desert, until she was close enough to the outpost to hear the chatter of illagers. Zetta couldn't understand what they were saying, but they seemed aggravated. Even more so than usual. Were they still humiliated by the beating they'd taken from her friends and neighbors? Probably. This raid would be several times larger than the last. There must have been several different clans present, all set on decimating Zetta's little town. Sienna Dunes would be torn apart in minutes.

Zetta kept her eyes open for something that would make good proof. She saw a chest filled with axes and crossbows, but those things were easy enough for anybody to craft. A banner would be perfect. There was one leaning up against the stone wall of the outpost, decorated with an angry gray face and beady blue eyes. But as soon as she took a few steps toward it, one of the raiders grabbed it and hoisted it up overhead. So much for that idea. Well, maybe a ravager harness would work? Zetta didn't think anyone would be able to craft one of those, and no way would anyone be willing to re-create that distinctly awful ravager smell . . . kind of like the smell at the bottom of a moldy compost bin, but so much worse.

There were several ravagers milling about behind a fence, all of them distracted by the comings and goings of the illagers. Zetta walked slowly and silently to their pen, coming within inches of an illager dressed differently from the others, wearing a long black robe with a band of gold running down the front of it. He just stood there, like he was in a trance, arms crossed in front of him.

Weird, Zetta thought, but she pressed past him. As she did, his head turned quickly toward her, and his eyes widened and seemed to be drilling right at Zetta. A scream nearly escaped her, but she swallowed it back down. She bit down on her knuckle and kept walking, sure that her invisibility potion was still working, though she didn't want to risk being here longer than she needed to be.

She arrived at the ravager pen, and when she was sure no one was watching, she unlatched the gate and slipped inside. There were five ravagers, their enormous hooves tearing up the dirt below them. Zetta had to remind herself that even though she was invisible, she wasn't invincible, and there were ten pointed horns among the beasts, any of which could impale her.

She decided one of the beasts seemed more docile than the others, though that was a bit like picking the least explosive creeper out of a group. The ravager could still trample her if it spooked, so she slowly worked the first buckle of the harness loose, then the next. She was then able to slide it off and let it fall gently to the dirt. She looked around cautiously now. To anyone who'd seen anything, it would have looked like the harness had simply come undone and slipped off. She waited a few more seconds, then started to slide the harness away from the beast's feet, very slowly, almost at a creep. A harness moving on its own would definitely draw suspicion.

Finally, Zetta folded the harness up tight and stuffed it under her shirt, within the protection of her invisibility potion. Then she started back the way she'd come. She was nearly halfway back to safety when a horn trumpeted. The illagers all jumped to attention and gathered around the one that was holding a large banner.

The raid captain, maybe? Though she couldn't understand what it was saying, it spoke with force and conviction. The other raiders nodded and harrumphed in agreement. They all sounded angry and bloodthirsty.

One good thing was that since all the illagers' attention was drawn to the captain, it was easier for Zetta to sneak out than it was to sneak in, which was great, because the ravager harness was bulky and kept slipping, and Zetta was really afraid she was going to drop it and blow her cover.

Just a few more steps, Zetta thought, right as a witch passed in front of her. The witch stopped dead in her tracks, then howled at her. Zetta thought she'd turned visible again, but her arms and legs were still nowhere to be seen. Still, the witch must have sensed her, or maybe sensed the potion on her—those faint, nearly invisible magic particles giving her away. Next thing Zetta knew, the witch was hurling a bottle at her. It splashed at her feet, and Zetta took off in a sprint. She didn't have far to run, but it felt like her legs were being held to the ground as she moved. She was still going forward, just very, very slowly.

Argh. A slowness potion. And the next potion the witch was getting ready to throw looked like something a lot deadlier. Zetta ducked as the witch threw it, and the potion landed wide, splashing in the sand. Zetta kept running, ducking and dodging as she could.

Now other illagers were alerted to her presence, and arrows buzzed past her ears. But finally, the slowness released its grip on her, and she found temporary safety behind the sandy hill. She hopped on the dragon's back and lifted it into the air and flew away as fast as the dragon could. She had her proof.

Zetta headed back toward Sienna Dunes, but she couldn't show up with the dragon there. She needed somewhere safe to hide it. Somewhere where no one would dare look. As the Great Rift that tore through the desert came into view, Zetta got an idea. A very bad idea, but it would have to do.

The old desert pyramid that Rift had shown her over a week ago was half buried in the side of the cliff, difficult to navigate on foot, but not so bad with a dragon. She landed the dragon there, hoping the sudden weight wouldn't send the whole structure careening into the lava river below.

The pyramid was in shambles, the half-missing wall in the front just wide enough for the dragon to fit through. After centuries of being abandoned, who knew what lurked inside? Now Zetta was about to find out. She lit a torch and stepped over the crumbling threshold that had once been the front door.

The dragon crept in behind her, crouched like a timid pup.

"We can't both be scared," Zetta told it.

The dragon snorted at her, nudging her forward into the room when her feet wouldn't go any farther. It looked like the room had been blown to smithereens a long time ago, and there was a large crater in the sandstone floor. Looters, probably. Looking for treasure. There wasn't any to be had anymore, but this big room would be comfortable enough to house a dragon for a bit.

Zetta heard the skitter of spiders in the dark corners where her torchlight didn't reach. She killed the first without a problem, but a second one snuck up on her without warning. It was about to bite her, when the dragon smashed it with one of its huge paws. Then it sniffed at the thing and recoiled.

"Good dragon," Zetta said. "We're going to need you to do that about a hundred more times, judging from the size of that raid coming for us. Now listen. I need you to stay right here. Don't move. Don't go anywhere, do you hear me?"

The dragon made a purring sound, then nuzzled the side of its head against Zetta's body.

"A horn scritch? Is that what you want? Okay, you saved me, so I guess that's worth a scritch." She gave the dragon a quick scratch behind the gray horns poking up from the top of its head, then sighed. She'd managed to not think of the dragon as a pet so far, like she'd planned. Only problem was, now she was starting to think of it as a *friend*.

Dragon purred again, then licked the side of her face. It wasn't quite as awful as she'd imagined.

"I'll be back soon. Remember: Don't go anywhere!" Zetta said as she backed out of the room slowly, making sure the dragon didn't follow her. It appeared like it was staying. Good. She kept her smile tight on her face, watching as the dragon's tail smacked gently against the rubble-ridden floor. She didn't want it to have any inkling of just how scared she was right now.

Then she was on her way back up the cliffside, using her pick-axe to staircase her way up as quickly as she could, ignoring the bits of stone falling past her and down into the lava river at the bottom of the ravine. Finally she was back on solid ground. She ran as quickly as she could, adrenaline instead of a swiftness potion fueling her, and going nearly as fast, even while carrying the bulky ravager harness.

The rift canyon ran through the desert, but it didn't feel nearly as deep as the one that ran between Zetta and her father. She needed to start there, before she made her way to the mayor. She needed her father on her side, and that meant she finally needed to tell him the truth.

The town came into view. No sign of the raid yet. The illagers had quite a way to travel. Hopefully that meant the people of Sienna Dunes would have enough time to prepare.

Zetta knocked on her front door, hoping her father was here and not off trying to hunt down the dragon. It felt odd, asking permission to enter her own home, but after all she'd been through, she was feeling more like a stranger here than ever. Her father answered, face stern.

"The mayor's been looking for you," he said, more of a grumble. "Someone has to be responsible for the damage that beast caused. I won't even ask—"

"You don't have to ask, Dad, because I'm going to tell you. Everything."

Her father took a deep breath, then stepped to the side so Zetta could come in. She looked him in the eyes and told him everything. From her early brewing attempts, to running off to visit her aunt for help with her potions, to cracking the ender dragon egg. He winced at that part and didn't stop wincing as her story went on. With everything coming out of her mouth like that, Zetta started to understand how much danger she'd put herself in. How much danger she'd put everyone in.

"You fought endermen?" her father asked.

Zetta nodded, though she hadn't put up much of a fight.

"You snuck into a pillager outpost?" He was holding the ravager harness now. He lifted it to his nose, scrunching his whole face up as he got a whiff of the gnarly smell. No way could he deny what she was saying.

She nodded again.

"And now you're telling me that the beast that nearly destroyed our town is ready to defend it?"

She nodded once more, seeing her opportunity. "We trained the ender dragon really well, and it could help us fight the raiders. They're coming. Maybe a hundred of them. We have to convince the mayor to get ready. Rift, Rayne, Ashton, and I—I know we're young, but we've got a lot of great ideas."

"If by 'ideas' you mean dragons that aren't supposed to exist and other magical non—"

"It's not magical nonsense, Dad. It's just the way the world works. And our world is changing. And yeah, some of the change is scary, but there's also opportunity to explore and create and reimagine how we want to live our lives. Mom knew that. Aunt Meryl knows that. What we can't do is hide our heads in the sand and hope the change passes us by. We need to act now!"

Her father was quiet for a long, long time. They didn't have time for this much silence, but Zetta had learned that sometimes things couldn't be rushed. This was a lot for her father to process all at once.

"Okay," he finally said. He walked over to the closet, unlocked it, then pulled out chests until the trapdoor was once again exposed. He popped a button next to the trapdoor and opened it. The chest hidden inside gleamed; Zeta figured he must have polished it. Zetta's father pulled the brewing stand out and handed it to Zetta. She was about to thank him profusely when he pulled something else out of the chest. A small, silver star.

Zetta blinked a few times. "What is that?" she asked. But something in her head clicked, and she knew. Still, she wanted to let her father be the one to say it out loud.

"It's a nether star. The one your mother got from the wither she killed. She'd talked about making a beacon from it to allow our miners to work with more haste. Maybe you can figure out how to use it. I'm assuming you took her book of inventions."

Zetta nodded. "I'm sorry. I should have asked."

"It's fine. She would have wanted you to have it. If she could see how brave and determined you were, she'd be proud." He smiled. "I'm proud of you."

Zetta's heart knocked in her chest as she heard those words. They were as precious as the nether star. She stared at the gleaming star as he placed it in her hands.

Now they just needed to get Mayor Maxine on board.

CHAPTER TWENTY

"No, absolutely not. We are not using magic to defend ourselves. Especially magic from the likes of you." The mayor pointed at Zetta, as if there were a doubt about whom she could be mad at.

Sheesh, Zetta thought. *You turn someone half invisible one time, and it's like they can't forgive you. And, well, there was that whole out-of-control-dragon-pretending-to-be-a-parade-float thing, too, but honestly, who hasn't messed up big-time at least once or twice in their life?*

"Zetta's telling the truth," Zetta's father said, tossing the ravager harness down in front of the mayor's feet. "She risked her own life to get proof so you would believe her. We have to use whatever means we have. If we don't, this may be the end of Sienna Dunes."

"The wall will protect us," Mayor Maxine said. "And I'll rally Captain Zayden and the fighters, and send archers to the watchtowers. Zetta's bravery is noted, but we can't have kids running around thinking they can save the whole Overworld!"

"I'm not trying to save the whole Overworld," Zetta said, refusing to back down from the mayor's glare. "I'm just trying to help this town. I'm a part of it, and it's a part of me. Isn't that enough?"

Mayor Maxine gritted her teeth, but her eyes were softening. "It's not that easy. The people of Sienna Dunes won't like this at all. We don't do magic here."

"Aren't you the mayor? The people trust you. They'll listen to you." Zetta stared hard at the mayor, eyes pleading for her to do the right thing. This was it. The moment of truth. Zetta's heart thudded in her chest. The mayor had to believe her.

"Fine—what do you need?" Mayor Maxine finally asked.

"We need to go into the town vault," Zetta said, flipping through her mother's notebook to the page showing a beacon mounted upon a pyramid made of various precious blocks. Iron. Emeralds. Gold. Diamonds. "We're going to need all the ore blocks we can get."

But the mayor was already shaking her head. "We can't waste—"

"There's not going to be anything to waste if we don't save our town," Zetta said, cutting her off. "My mother has instructions on what to do. We can grant extra strength, and maybe even regeneration effects, if we can build this pyramid high enough."

"Fine," the mayor relented. "What else?"

"I'll need some blaze powder for potions and to craft some more brewing stands. I can make potions for arrows and general use. We'll need lots of glass bottles. Lots of water. Rift can construct an automated arrow-firing machine. And a TNT cannon . . ." Zetta winced at that last part, but kept pushing through with her demands. "We'll need materials for those, too. Rift can help you set up several along the wall. Do you have others who can help?"

Mayor Maxine didn't even balk at the enormity of the request. She finally seemed to be taking Zetta seriously and called in Captain Zayden to divide up the assignments among his fighters. They were a ragtag crew, miners and builders and vendors all coming together to make this plan of Zetta's work. Cora, the blacksmith, donated all the axes and swords in her shop to whoever needed them.

And of course, the ender dragon would ensure they were successful, but Zetta kept quiet about that, since she didn't want to press her luck any further with the mayor just yet.

Back in the town hall, Zetta followed Mayor Maxine to the vault doors. The mayor had Zetta look the other way while she fed a secret object into the chest nearby, and as the chest squeaked shut, Zetta heard the faintest sound of redstone contraptions clicking behind the wall, analyzing the object to make sure it was the correct one to grant access to the vault.

Finally, Zetta watched rapt as the piston doors retracted, revealing the contents of the vault. Zetta felt more than a little pride that her mother's invention had kept the town's ores safe from the raiders. Dozens of chests lined the walls, labeled with everything that the town held precious. Zetta looked at her drawing again. They needed 164 mineral blocks to build a four-level pyramid.

Several assistants started pulling iron ingots from the chests and crafting them into blocks as the mayor continued to take stock.

"We're going to be short," she said to Zetta. "But don't worry—if I know this town, we'll find a way to make it happen. I'll go door to door asking for ingots if I have to."

Zetta breathed a sigh of relief now that Mayor Maxine was fully on board. The mayor loaded Zetta down with blaze rods to turn into powder. Zetta then ran to fetch her friends and her cousin, but they were already at the stairs leading up to the town hall when she stepped outside.

"We heard the news," Rift said.

"Illagers are coming. Lots of them," said Rayne.

"Where's the dragon?" asked Ashton.

"Safe," Zetta said. "At the Great Rift, in the old desert pyramid. I want you to fetch it, but Rayne will have to show you how to get there. And, yeah, the raid is huge. But we've got this. We just need everyone to work together. Once you've got the dragon, keep it in the barn until I give the word."

"We can do it!" Ashton shouted, before dragging Rayne off toward the north end of town.

"Rift, I need you to get some builders to construct at least four of your arrow-shooting contraptions along the wall. A TNT cannon, too. Captain Zayden can help you figure out the most strategic places to put them."

"Can do, boss," Rift said with a tip of his head. And then Zetta was left on her own.

Zetta returned to the vault and crafted eight brewing stands.

She'd had trouble keeping up with half as many, but making as many potions as possible was really important. The mayor's assistants kept delivering her water-filled bottles, one after another, faster than Zetta needed them. She worked hard and diligently, making notes so she kept her focus sharp and didn't get distracted.

She started with the lingering potions. She took out all of her dragon's breath and fell into a groove, first brewing poison potions, then ones for harming and weakness. When the lingering potions were done, she fussed about with them on a crafting table, arranging arrows in different ways until, at last, the tips changed colors and started emitting magic particles. No time to celebrate, though. She handed the petite glass bottles off to the assistants along with her crafting recipe so they could use them to make more tipped arrows. If the smell of dozens of fermented spider eyes bothered anyone, no one said anything.

It took over an hour to get a couple hundred tipped arrows made. When Zetta ran out of dragon's breath, she started making splash potions as well. She knew she wouldn't be much use in hand-to-hand combat, but she could lob potions like the best of them and her aim was more than decent. Then she shoved all the arrows she could carry into her pack and had the assistants carry the rest as she made her way back out into the town square.

The arrow turrets were nearly complete. Zetta distributed the arrows to each of the firing contraptions, but she didn't have time to stick around and watch as they were loaded in. She passed the rest of her potions to Captain Zayden, and he took them gratefully.

"You've really done an amazing job, Zetta," Captain Zayden said.

"Thanks. I hope the tipped arrows are helpful."

"They will be. And this will be, too." Captain Zayden pulled an enchanted bow from his pack. "As long as you have one arrow, you have infinite arrows. I only had enough experience to make a few. Please give this one to your friend. And try not to break it this time."

Zetta took the bow and carefully placed it in her pack. She promised herself she wouldn't take it out again until she was standing in front of Rayne, not even if a dozen ravagers were threatening to trample her.

The beacon was nearly finished being constructed near the east wall. Cora the blacksmith strained as she carried a solid gold block up to the fourth and final layer and placed it down with a thud. She wiped the sweat from her brow, then stepped aside as Zetta's father placed the final piece—it looked like a glass block, except it had the nether star caught inside, shining brilliantly like a diamond. And just like that, the beacon was finished.

A vertical beam of white light shot straight up into the sky, slowly rotating around and around. Everyone was mesmerized, but as the shock of the beacon's beauty began to wear off, Zetta noticed that she really didn't feel any different. Not stronger. Not faster.

She jumped in place, but barely got off the ground, just like always.

Nothing had changed.

"It's not working," Cora called down to Zetta. "I think we're missing a step."

"What do you mean, it's not working?" Zetta said, scaling the pyramid. The polished precious blocks were slippery beneath her boots. She stepped up carefully, then stood beside Cora as they both looked at the diagram in Zetta's mother's notebook. It seemed as if everything was set up correctly. Zetta flipped the page, but it was the last one in the notebook. "Umm . . ."

Zetta felt pressure mounting in her chest. Everyone was staring at her, expecting her to know what to do. She could figure it out. She just needed time. Unfortunately, that was the one thing she didn't have. From up here on top of the pyramid, she could see right over the barrier wall.

The raid had arrived, close enough that Zetta could just barely make out the scowls on the gray faces. The raid captain carried their pillager banner high, and she could feel the pyramid slightly trembling under her feet as the ravagers stomped forward in unison. The raid horn trumpeted, announcing the illagers' attack. All was so silent within the great wall surrounding Sienna Dunes that Zetta could hear her heart beating like a pickaxe smashing stone.

CHAPTER
TWENTY-ONE

Seconds later, the bell tower starting ringing. Things had seemed so orderly a few minutes ago with everyone working together to prepare for the raid, but now everything devolved into chaos. Screaming and crying came from all directions, and Captain Zayden's ragtag army had trouble keeping in formation.

Benjamin the slime harvester dropped his sword twice, like he'd forgotten how to use it. Zetta imagined he must have slayed thousands of slime cubes over the years, and now here he was, his nerves completely rattled.

Zetta understood, though. Slow-bouncing cubes of slime really weren't that big of a threat, and they were certainly easy to outrun if one got surrounded. But there was no outrunning the threat that was on their horizon. Over a hundred illagers and their band of hostile mobs were steadily walking toward Sienna Dunes. It was almost like a slow-motion wreck, giving everyone within the town plenty of time to worry and wonder and panic.

Rayne and Ashton arrived a few minutes later, panting and out of breath.

"We can't find the dragon," Ashton said, his voice cracking. Zetta could see the pain in his deep brown eyes. "We looked everywhere. We called for it. It's gone."

"Oh no. Maybe it went looking for you again," Zetta said, laying a hand on her cousin's shoulder to comfort him. She turned her head up to the sky, hoping that at this very moment, the dragon would swoop down and spray the entire raid in its purple poison. She didn't want to admit that there was an equal chance that it had gotten fed up with being left behind and tricked and chased, and had flown off in search of a quieter life. A life that didn't involve a group of well-meaning friends and a town that wanted to hunt it down.

"Yeah, probably," Ashton said. He didn't sound any more convinced than Zetta was.

"We'll have to do the best we can without it," Zetta said. She handed Rayne her last poison arrow.

Rayne's smile was thin. "Just one?" they asked, examining the arrow. The arrowhead was green instead of white, and tiny magic particles glistened in the air around it. "I was expecting at least a dozen or so."

"One is all you'll need," Zetta said, pulling the enchanted bow out next and quickly handing it over before she found some unexpected way to destroy it.

Rayne looked like they were going to faint. "An enchanted bow? Thank you!"

"Thank Captain Zayden. Later. Right now, we've got a town to defend, and I still need to figure out how to get that beacon working. The instructions just stop, but I know my mother took great notes. I know this isn't a mistake."

"Umm . . ." Ashton said, pulling out his notebook and opening it up. "You probably want to look at this . . ."

Zetta shooed him away. "Sorry, Ashton. I don't have time for your mob sketches right now."

"It's not a mob sketch." He pushed the page in front of Zetta. It wasn't a mob sketch. It was a sketch of the beacon, with instructions on how to activate it.

Zetta flipped Ashton's old notebook closed. It was nearly identical to her mother's. "Where'd you get this?"

"Found it in your closet a couple years ago when you were babysitting me. Or supposed to be babysitting me. You fell asleep."

Zetta shook her head, but she didn't have time to be exasperated by her little cousin. She sprinted over to her dad and handed him the notebook. He took it, read the page over, and then fed an iron ingot into the beacon.

A hard breeze whipped past Zetta, like a magical shockwave that made her eyes flutter. Not soon after, she felt the familiar gift of strength, only this time it felt more natural. There wasn't that deep desire to show off. She was simply filled with a need to do the most good she could with this extra boost.

Rift ran over to his contraptions, and Rayne climbed the rickety ladder up to the top of one of the watchtowers. As everyone took their places, Zetta looked at Ashton. Without the dragon to command, he didn't really have anything to do. "Ashton, why don't you help the mayor gather up everyone who's not fighting and get them into the vault. Especially Nana and Papa. You know how stubborn they are."

He sighed and nodded, then took off.

"I thought you said there were about a hundred of them," Rayne called from the watchtower, arrow notched, eyes trained hard on their bow sight.

"There were," Zetta said, climbing up to join them. She quickly estimated the enemy's numbers from her spot in the tower. There seemed to be closer to two hundred illagers now, and nearly a dozen ravagers were among the enemy mobs. "They must have had some other clans join them."

"That's okay," Rayne said. "Our plan is still solid. It just might take a little longer."

Zetta nodded, like she believed this. They had infinite hope. Infinite faith. And now they had infinite arrows. The fight would be tough, but they were as prepared as they could be. Plus, the mob was about to walk right into the blast path of the TNT cannon.

"Rift, are you ready?" Captain Zayden called from the next tower over.

"Yes, sir!" Rift yelled from his spot next to the cannon. Zetta still couldn't believe the mayor had approved it. Somehow, it made her feel ill knowing the mayor thought they were so desperate. "Just say the word!"

In the next instant, the captain swiped his hand down and yelled, "Fire TNT cannons!"

Rift lit the double-barreled cannon, then stepped back as the red TNT sticks started flashing. Almost simultaneously, two TNT blocks were expelled from the contraption at a tremendous speed, heading straight for the mob. The illagers didn't have time to react to the attack. The TNT exploded right on contact, perfectly timed. A cloud of dust and debris filled the air. Everyone in the towers cheered, but as the sandy haze started to dissipate, the townspeople saw that the raid was still heavy in number. The TNT cannons should have had a bigger effect than that. They'd landed perfectly.

Zetta couldn't understand what had gone wrong, until she saw the pointed black hats in the raid, surrounded by a thick fog of red particles. Witches. They were tossing splash potions left and right to heal their ranks.

"Fire TNT cannons!" Captain Zayden said again.

Again, the cannons fired flawlessly, but this time the raiders were ready. They'd spread out. The cannons decimated another twenty illagers, but the rest of the raid held steady. The third TNT shot sailed right over their heads, doing minimal damage. Rift looked dejected, head hanging low. Maybe the cannon hadn't been as effective as he'd hoped. But it had still done damage, and those illagers had to be scared. That was worth something.

The raiders were now too close to attempt another shot from the cannon, but that meant they were in range of the best archers.

Rayne let off three arrows, each sinking into its target, an enraged vindicator. Right as the third arrow landed, the vindicator blinked away in a puff of smoke. "Nice shot," Zetta said, noticing Rayne was using regular arrows. "But what happened to the poison-tipped arrows?"

"The infinity shot doesn't work on tipped arrows, but this bow is so powerful, I don't even need them," Rayne said, voice full of determination. They notched another arrow. "One down, only a hundred and fifty or so left to go."

"Aim for the ones with weapons first," Captain Zayden said. "Ready the arrow launcher!"

Zetta didn't want to disturb her friend further, so she looked over at Rift, who was now racing to the control panel of his arrow launcher. There were four levers, one to control each launcher. He pulled the lever to activate all four of the contraptions. Trails of red dust glowed, then moments later, the firing started. Arrows flew out at an alarming pace, so many of them, Zetta couldn't follow a single one. They started landing, but since the raiders were so spread out, they ended up striking the ground more often than the enemy.

The pillagers were close enough to return fire, their crossbows aimed high at the towers. An arrow whizzed past Zetta and stuck into the roof of the tower. Another hit her in the shoulder. Before she could yell out in pain, she felt the effects of the beacon wash over her like a warm bath, and instantly she was healed. She plucked the arrow from her arm, and tossed it aside, unbothered.

Now the raiders were close enough that even the greenest archers with the most minimal skills were hitting their targets. Zetta was able to start tossing poison splash potions, but with the witches doing the same with healing potions, the effects were canceled out.

Instead of wasting another potion, Zetta sat back and took time to really observe their enemy. Captain Zayden had ordered the archers to take out the raiders with weapons first, which was leaving those weird illagers in the robes virtually untouched. But as Zetta looked deep into their mesmerizing green eyes, she knew this decision had been a mistake.

"We need to target those illagers in the robes," she called out to Captain Zayden. "They're up to something. I can feel it." Why else would they seem so at ease in the face of so much fighting?

Captain Zayden looked out into the surge of raiders, and he must have seen it, too, the calm on their gray faces hiding the danger those crossed arms held. "Change of plans," he barked to his fighters. "Take out the illagers in the robes first!" He glanced back at Zetta, a look of awe on his face. "Good call, Zetta. If you ever need a favor from me, just say the—"

"They're summoning something!" screamed one of the fighters. The robed illagers had stopped their march and had lifted their arms, waving them about in big circles. Fanged teeth erupted from the ground, some of them traveling under the wall and biting at the fighters standing nearby. Zetta had never seen anything like it. Those hungry maws surged up from nowhere, ready for flesh. Ready for vengeance. The townspeople were terrified, but the beacon had them regenerating and healed up in no time.

The robed illagers began summoning again, and suddenly,

the air was filled with a flock of pale gray birds that started dive-bombing the towers. Not birds, Zetta saw as they got closer, but creepy little winged demons carrying the tiniest of swords. They were so small, Zetta almost forgot to be afraid of them, but then one of them swooped in and smacked her in the forehead with its sword, which, though tiny, hurt like the full-sized version.

"Ow!" she shouted, swatting the thing away like an insect. But more were coming. She pulled out an axe from her pack and starting hacking away at them, trying to vanquish the little nuisances quickly so Rayne and the other archers wouldn't be distracted. One of them nicked Rayne in the back, causing them to misfire their bow and nearly hit Captain Zayden in the next tower over.

"Sorry!" Rayne shouted. Rayne and the other archers spent the next few moments picking the vexing creatures from the sky with well-placed arrows. Then Rayne took aim at a robed illager who was in the middle of casting another spell. The arrows ripped right through that gold-trimmed robe, and soon, the illager was no more.

But there were many, many more of them. And now they were next to the wall.

"My bow's down to half durability," Rayne yelled, exasperated.

"Already?" Zetta said. She checked each of the chests in the tower. The potions were running low, too. She grabbed one. "Let's work together then. I'll toss, you aim and take out the weakened enemies before the witches get a chance to heal them."

Rayne nodded, and together the friends started picking off the other robed mobs, until screams started coming from the ground below. Zetta rushed to the side of the tower and looked down. A small army was gathered close to the wall, prepared to defend the area in case of a breach, but now they were in a panic as fanged mouths punctured through the sand again and snapped at their feet.

Zetta shook her head, then lobbed more potions at the robed illagers. There were only a few of them left now. Rayne finished them off, but not even a second later, one of the ravagers crashed through their terracotta wall.

Terracotta chunks rained down, creating an abstract mosaic of color in the sand. Zetta would have thought it pretty, if it hadn't spelled certain doom for the people of Sienna Dunes.

Fighting broke out beneath the tower. Captain Zayden shouted out orders and somehow got the frazzled army back into ranks. They drew their stone swords and battled witches and pillagers and vindicators and ravagers. For a moment, it looked like they were holding their own, but more and more mobs continued to spill through the opening in the wall. The beacon was helping, but it could only do so much as the fighting started to spread out past the range of its effects.

Zetta dropped the last few healing and regeneration potions she had on Captain Zayden and his fighters, and it was helping, but even with the beacon's strength boost, it soon became obvious that she was just delaying the inevitable. No one had wanted to say it out loud, but they were simply outnumbered and outmatched.

"Retreat!" yelled Captain Zayden. The word was simple, but it ripped a hole in Zetta's soul. Maybe her hope wasn't infinite after all.

The tower shook beneath her feet. She looked down again, and this time saw a ravager ramming its head into the base of the tower. It was made of brittle terracotta, too, and wouldn't hold forever. In fact, as the floor beneath Zetta had already started to crack, she wasn't even sure if it would hold the next few seconds.

Then the floor wasn't beneath her at all, just terracotta dust and air, and the next thing she knew, the tower was collapsing, and she was falling with it.

CHAPTER
TWENTY-TWO

Everything was black. Everything hurt. Zetta felt the debris around her shifting. Then the broken blocks above her were being lifted away. Soon she felt cool air on her face and hands tugging her to safety. She hoped they were tugging her to safety.

"I've got you." It was Rift's voice. "We're retreating to the vault. We'll be safe in there."

He sounded defeated, but Zetta knew they'd be safe in the vault. The walls were made of iron blocks, and not even an enraged ravager could pound its way through it. Zetta wiped the dust and gunk from her eyes. When she opened them, she saw Rift staring at her. Rayne was right behind him, bloody and scraped up, but otherwise okay.

Together, the friends slipped away toward the town hall, trying to ignore the destruction and the cries of the last line of fighters going up against impossible odds, swinging their swords at the endless raid so they could buy time for the rest of the townspeople to get to safety.

The friends ambled up the stairs of the town hall, then went to the back of the building where the vault was. The doors were wide open, and the whole town was crammed inside.

"Where's Ashton?" was Zetta's first clear thought. Inside, family members were seeking one another out. Zetta shook off the pain in her bones and stood on her tiptoes, looking over heads in hopes of spotting Ashton.

Over the din of frantic conversation, Zetta could still hear Captain Zayden calling for retreat. He was getting closer now. That was that. The fighting was over. Sienna Dunes was there for the illagers' taking. Would they steal their valuables? Destroy their buildings? Would they ever leave?

Finally, Zetta let out a sigh of relief as she saw her cousin. He was looking frantic, even for someone who'd just been through an attack.

"Ashton!" Zetta screamed out. She ran over and pulled him into a tight hug. "Are you okay?"

He shook his head. "No. I mean, I'm fine. But I can't find Nana and Papa. They should have been here. They said they were coming when I went to the farm to fetch them and sent me ahead. But I've looked. So many times. They're not here. Your dad's not here either."

Dad could still possibly be held up with Captain Zayden and the other fighters, but Ashton was right: Nana and Papa should have already been in the vault.

Captain Zayden arrived, ushering in the last of the fighters. Zetta's father was not among them. The mayor started to pull the lever to close the iron block doors.

"Wait!" Zetta said to Mayor Maxine. "My grandparents and father, they're not in here."

"We can't wait," the mayor replied, her voice soft and full of remorse, even in this time of terror. "We gave warnings. We have to close the doors now."

Zetta knew how stubborn her grandparents were. She had a feeling they wouldn't leave their farm. It had been their home for decades, and no way would they give it up without a fight. Zetta and Ashton exchanged looks. They both knew what they had to do.

"We're going to the farm," Zetta whispered to Rift and Rayne. "Our grandparents are still there."

"How are we going to get past the illagers?" Rift asked, bouncing up and down, raring to go.

"We?" Zetta asked.

"I'm not letting you go alone."

"Same," said Rayne. "But we need to figure out the logistics later." Rayne pointed at the iron doors, the pistons extending with a series of mechanical-sounding *clunks* to push them closed again. The friends all made a run for it, slipping past the doors right before they shut tight with a slam that quaked Zetta's bones.

"I'm out of potions," Zetta said. She dared to peek through the door to the town hall. Dozens and dozens of illagers were still about, ransacking the entire town. Looting stores, burning down homes. It was like they were thirsty for revenge. Even if she'd had an invisibility potion on her, she didn't think it'd be safe to go out there.

She peeked into her pack anyway, hoping she'd overlooked something. All she had left in there was Meechie the shovel, and her iron pickaxe. She pulled out her pickaxe. "If we can't sneak past them, we'll just have to go under them."

Zetta started digging right there through the sandstone floor of the town hall. She dug down to several blocks, then started swinging as fast as she could in a straight line toward the farm. For a few minutes, she felt the powerful hum of the beacon in her bones, but it faded as they grew closer to the farm and far out of the beacon's range. Her arms ached now, but she didn't let that slow her down. Her friends crowded in behind her. It was dark, and she couldn't see anything, but it was important that she concentrate.

How many blocks had they traveled? Fifty? Sixty? Zetta tried to keep a tally as she mined, so thankful for her recent training. So thankful she had this iron axe instead of a stone one. She fell into a trance, letting the rhythm of mining soothe her worn nerves, just like Milo had taught her. Ninety-eight. Ninety-nine. One hundred.

They had to have gone far enough now. Zetta went a few more blocks, just to be sure, then popped up to get her bearings. She hit dirt instead of sand, which was a good sign. Sure enough, she came up in a wheat field. Perfect cover, since she heard illagers milling about. But only a few.

"How's your bow?" Zetta asked.

"About done for," Rayne groaned.

"Well, hopefully it'll last a few more shots. I need you to take out those three illagers by the carrots. Then we can make a run for Nana and Papa's place."

Rayne nodded, taking careful aim. They couldn't afford to miss even one shot. Two of the illagers went down, but the bow broke on their third attempt. That illager was on high alert now and would warn the others if they didn't take it out.

"I've got this," Rift said, sword drawn. Zetta nodded, biting back her own urge to run out there. Her arms were the consistency of slime cubes from all the mining anyway. Rift came back thirty seconds later, shoulders hunched, still a little glum. "Done. At least I got that right. Let's move."

The friends ran toward Nana and Papa's place. Zetta was sprinting, and barely had the breath to spare, but she ran up beside Rift. "Don't be mad about the TNT cannon. You did your best."

"Nah, could have done better," Rift said back. "A lot better. Those arrow-firing contraptions weren't great either."

"They helped," Zetta said. "And next time we'll know to—"

"There might not be a next time," Rift said. "Because of me."

Zetta wanted to console her friend, but as they got closer to the front porch, a plate flew out the window, nearly knocking Ashton in the head. "Nana! Papa!" he said. "It's us! Let us in!"

A bowl flew out the window this time, hitting Rift in the shoulder. "Ouch!" he cried.

"How do we know you aren't pillagers trying to trick us!" hollered Papa. "We saw those magical spells! You could be in our heads!"

"I can name every pet chicken we ever had!" Ashton called out. "Could a pillager do that! There's Mauve and Three Feathers, and Earline and Tucker, and Salma and Nella, and—"

The door swung open, and Nana yanked Ashton in by the collar. "What are you doing outside yelling like that? Don't you know we're in the middle of a raid?"

"But, Nana—"

"Don't 'but Nana' me, sir." Then, "Get on in here," Nana yelled at the rest of them. Zetta and her friends hustled inside.

"Is Dad here?" Zetta asked.

Papa nodded. "He tried to get us to come to the vault, but we said we're staying here and protecting the farm. We're not surrendering!" He picked up a raw potato. "Not as long as I've got strength in my arm and breath in my lungs and can throw one of these!"

"He's out there in the beetroot field now, collecting seeds!" Nana added, grabbing a stone hoe and gripping it like a sword. "He says he'll collect enough for us to start over. We don't want to start over! I won't stand by and watch those beasts trample years of hard work!"

Nana took a couple of wild swings, nearly knocking Ashton in the head. Ashton backed up to the wall, giving her plenty of space.

The front door opened, and Papa threw three potatoes at the intruder, hard and fast. Zetta was impressed.

"It's just me!" came her father's voice. He walked in, rubbing his forehead where Zetta was sure a potato-shaped bruise would be forming very soon. "I've got your seeds. We need to get to the town hall where we'll be safe."

Zetta nodded. "I mined a path from the town hall to the farm. Right through all the sandstone. It's a straight shot." The vault doors were closed, but maybe Dad could convince the mayor to open them again.

Dad arched an eyebrow. "You mined all the way here?"

"You should have seen her," Ashton said. "She was a mining machine!"

"Our straight shot isn't so straight now," Rayne said, peering through the window. "Looks like we've got company. There're several illagers between us and our escape tunnel. All of them are armed."

Zetta looked out the window herself. Rayne was right. Five gray faces were milling around the entrance to the tunnel. Two of them had crossbows and the other three had axes. Not impossible odds. At least there weren't any ravagers or robed illagers or witches.

"Okay, what weapons do we have?" Zetta asked.

"My bow is broken," Rayne said.

"My sword is about to break," Rift said. "It's got a couple more swings in it, max."

"I've got hundreds of raw potatoes," Papa said, patting a barrel and standing proudly next to it like it was filled with TNT blocks and not a year's supply of spuds.

"I'm out of potions and my pickaxe is busted. All I've got left is Meechie." Zetta held up the shovel.

A pained look crossed Ashton's face. And Zetta felt the same pain in her heart. She didn't want to admit it, but she'd grown fond of the dragon. It had become a part of their little team, and now it was gone. She sighed. "Okay. So we're low on weapons, but we're not low on ideas. We've got one of the best pranksters on our side," she said, staring at Rift.

"Zetta, this isn't a time for Rift's antics," Father said, probably still sore about the time Rift had used double-extending pistons to lock him in the bathroom.

"You're wrong about that, Dad. Now is the perfect time," Zetta said. Maybe Rift's arrow launcher and TNT cannon hadn't worked out like they'd hoped, but there was one thing Rift did better than anyone else. Pranks and traps. Those illagers wouldn't know what hit them. "Okay, Rift. If you're looking for a chance to redeem yourself, it's time to do your thing!"

A smile crossed his face. The confidence he'd lost with the TNT explosion slowly seeped back into his body. "Pranks I can definitely do!" He turned to Nana. "Do you have any anvils?"

"A few," Nana said. "But most of them are all busted up."

"Doesn't matter. Bring them here," he commanded. Then, remembering his manners, Rift added, "Please, Nana Night?" He turned to Zetta's cousin. "Ashton, I need you to dig a pit in the sandy patch over by the carrot field."

Rift took the shovel from Zetta and handed it to Ashton, then continued giving out assignments until everyone was hustling about, gathering supplies from around the farm and creating traps for the illagers. Fifteen minutes later, they were ready and at their assigned stations. There were more illagers now; apparently, word had gotten out. The illagers were hungry for easy targets.

Not on Zetta's watch.

CHAPTER
TWENTY-THREE

Zetta didn't really appreciate being bait. But Rift was busy orchestrating this convoluted plan, and Dad and Rayne were still assembling their traps, and Papa was too slow and Nana had too quick of a temper, and no way would Zetta put Ashton in peril like this, so it had to be her.

She took her spot, careful not to step directly on the sand, then she shouted to a group of illagers, "Hey! Raiders! You missed an emerald!" She held up a shiny green stone, glimmering in the moonlight.

The illagers' eyes flashed. They let out a chorus of angry moans and harrumphs, then started toward her with their bows and axes raised. Fear shot through Zetta, and she almost forgot to move. She shook the feeling away, then dodged an arrow as it flew past her and into the fence post of the chicken coop. The chickens squawked and ruffled their feathers, but then continued strutting around like the world wasn't about to come to an end.

Zetta kept backing up. Kept dodging, wishing she had more than her mother's old leather boots for protection. Another arrow whooshed by her, but the pillagers were almost to the sand patch now. They stepped on the sandpit, and the sand did what sand does best.

It collapsed right under their feet.

The five illagers that had been leading the march fell into the trap. It wasn't far enough of a drop to kill them, but they wouldn't be getting out anytime soon. Zetta then made a run for the trough where the pigs were fed. It was a covered area with a low ceiling and open walls. The sandstone floor made it easy to clean. Now it was covered with pressure plates, maybe twenty in all, spaced all around in a maze of sorts.

Zetta stepped carefully, trying to remember the exact path Rift had given her—start at the fifth block from the right, go forward three blocks, left two, forward three. Right two. Or was it three?

Zetta stopped for a moment, trying to remember. She must have taken a wrong turn, because there were pressure plates all around her now, and there was no way to go but back. She felt her heart beat rapidly in her chest, but then she realized it was actually the hard footsteps of the approaching illagers. She didn't want to set off the trap, but she couldn't remember what to do next. It was only three more blocks between her and the dirt. She could make the jump, if she tried really hard.

Maybe.

Zetta backed up to the end of the block, did a little sprint, then launched herself as far as she could over the pressure plates. She landed on the other side of the trough, just as an arrow struck exactly where she'd been standing a moment before. Phew.

The angry illagers crossed into the trough area, but none of them noticed the pressure plates on the sandstone floor. Three of them stepped on a plate, and the four sandstone blocks surrounding them shot up from the ground, locking them in place. Two of them had axes and were no longer a threat, but one of them had a crossbow, and raised it right at Zetta and fired.

The arrow sunk into Zetta's thigh. She screamed out in pain.

The remaining illagers were bearing right down on Zetta, but then a potato hit one of them in the head. Another spud followed. The miffed raiders grunted and started off in the direction of the tuber attack, out toward the potato field.

Then Zetta heard an even louder scream coming from the porch of the main house. It was Nana. She had her hoe sharpened, iron gleaming. She charged at the pillager who had shot Zetta.

"Nana, don't!" Zetta screamed, but it was too late. Nana swung her hoe at the pillager. It tried to attack back, but Nana was too close. Nana smiled as the pillager vanished in a puff of smoke, leaving behind a crossbow and a few arrows. Nana picked them up, a wicked gleam in her eyes. Zetta was suddenly super-glad that Nana was on their side.

"Maybe you should give those to Rayne," Zetta suggested, wincing through the pain.

"Not a chance," Nana said. She took aim at one of the illagers that had gone off toward the potato field. Zetta saw Papa trying to run away, but he wasn't fast enough. The illagers were gaining on him. Nana fired, and the arrow sunk right into the illager's back. She fired a second arrow, and it poofed altogether.

Zetta watched as Nana dropped the crossbow, pulled her hoe out again, and ran over to attack the two remaining illagers. Papa continued to throw potatoes. Zetta didn't know whether to laugh or cry or just let the terror grip her. Nana finished those last two illagers off in no time. But when Zetta heard harrumphing coming from the direction of the barn, the smile fell completely off her face.

More illagers were coming this way.

"We need to get to the house!" Zetta said, scrambling up onto her feet. It hurt badly, but she was still able to walk. She wished the farm weren't so far away from the beacon. But she was slowly healing. She hobbled toward the house. She was so focused on getting to safety, she completely forgot to watch where she was stepping, until she heard a click as she reached to open the front door. Rift yanked her away just in time as three old anvils fell from the ceiling.

"So much for that trap," Rift said.

"Thanks," Zetta said. "But we're going to need a lot more than a few traps now." She pointed at the barn. Another twenty illagers were gathering there.

"Everyone, inside!" Rift called, ushering them all to the side entrance. Nana and Papa came running. Dad and Rayne too. Rift shut the door.

"Okay," Zetta said. "We're going to have to regroup and think of another way out of this. Maybe if we create a diversion—" Zetta looked around. "Wait, where's Ashton?"

Zetta ran to the window and froze in terror when she saw her cousin out there, trying to defend himself from the illagers with nothing but a shovel. "He's out there! We have to save him!"

Zetta forgot all about the pain in her leg, and she sprinted for the barn. She hoped she would make it there . . . and then what? Whack the illagers in the legs with wheat shafts? It didn't matter. She just needed to get there.

Suddenly, the air whipped and cracked like a rare desert storm was rolling in. The wheat in the field stirred slightly in the ominous breeze. But it never rained in Sienna Dunes, not in the town's entire history. Both Zetta and Ashton looked up as the sound of harsh flapping intensified, hoping beyond hope to see the black dragon against the backdrop of the night sky. Zetta could just make out the purple eyes blending in with the stars overhead. But they were moving. And getting closer.

She wanted to feel relief that the dragon was here to help them, but as the dragon swooped down, Zetta got a better appreciation for just how enormous and frightening it was. It was twice as big as before, and all traces of the pup she'd known were completely gone. Zetta's relief was quickly replaced by fear, and it sent a chill through her bones.

This was the most hostile mob of all hostile mobs.

"It molted again!" Zetta and Ashton said together.

The dragon breathed poison on the illagers farthest from Zetta and Ashton, the purple cloud causing them nonstop damage until they faded into nothingness. The dragon swooped down a second time, diving toward a pillager sinking arrow after arrow into that nearly impenetrable scaly hide. If it was hurt, the dragon didn't let on.

Instead, the dragon punched the pillager with its big black snout. The pillager let out an "Oof" and flew to the other side of the farm, landing in the pigpen and vanishing on impact.

The dragon's tail took out a few more pillagers and vindicators, leaving just a handful alive. Ashton held Meechie up, the shovel's handle blocking the blow of a vindicator's axe. The vindicator snarled at Ashton, then grabbed the shovel and broke it in half, leaving Ashton completely defenseless.

As the vindicator threw Meechie's remains to the ground, the dragon unleashed a cry of agony that rattled Zetta's eardrums and made her gut clench up. It was like the screech of a thousand rabid bats, rising in pitch until the windows on Nana and Papa's house shattered.

"Back up, Ashton," Zetta shouted to her cousin, but her voice was lost in the dragon's wailing.

"What?" Ashton shouted back.

The dragon's purple eyes inflamed as they trained on the vindicator that had broken its favorite toy. It huffed its nostrils, flapped up high into the air, then pulled its wings tight against its body as it descended again. Zetta noticed it wasn't slowing down. In fact, the dragon seemed to be picking up speed.

Zetta gestured for Ashton to move out of the way, and Ashton bolted, putting as much distance as he could between him and the dragon as it drove its snout right into the dirt.

The vindicator that had been standing there moments before was pounded into the ground, and the dragon didn't stop there. The whole wheat field became a pit of dirt as the dragon continued to cut through the earth. Finally, it pulled back up.

All the illagers at the farm were gone now, but the dragon still looked angry. Ashton ran over to what was left of Meechie, but it was just wood splinters now. He took a few steps toward the dragon, hand outstretched, but Zetta yanked him back.

"Absolutely not!" Zetta shouted at him. "Did you just see what—"

"It's Dragon," Ashton pleaded. "Our dragon."

Zetta shook her head. Maybe it was once, but no more. The dragon continued to rage, flying through the barn and leveling it. Finally, the dragon flapped off toward the horizon. The damage was great, but at least there had been no townspeople about. They were all held safely in the—

"Oh no," Zetta said, as the dragon turned back toward town. She couldn't be sure. She didn't want to be sure. But it seemed like the dragon was headed right for the town hall.

CHAPTER
TWENTY-FOUR

Zetta blinked, and by the time her eyes opened again, half of the town hall building was gone, ripped apart by the dragon's collision. Blocks of sandstone and terracotta flew everywhere, though the vault seemed to have held. Zetta watched as the dragon flew up into the air, those massive wings flapping so hard, she could feel the air currents churning from where she stood.

The dragon took aim at the remaining illagers that were still plundering and looting and picked them off one by one. It obliterated the belltower in the process, the last sad clang of brass filling Sienna Dunes with a harrowing off-key note. As the enraged beast drove its snout into the final raider, it left a giant scar of rubble and upturned sand through the once-bustling town square. The well was gone. Nothing was left intact. Dust and dirt filled Zetta's lungs. She coughed and struggled to breathe. She struggled to stand.

Yes, the pillager raid had been dealt with, but at what cost?

Before Zetta could even start to ponder such a painful question, she noticed the dragon making another slow turn as it headed back toward the town yet again. "Halt, Dragon," she muttered weakly. "Stop, Dragon!" she said, louder this time. The dragon's purple eyes slitted toward Zetta briefly, but then focused back on its target—the tattered shell of the town hall. The raiders were taken care of, but the dragon had no intention of stopping its attack. Zetta wanted to turn away. She couldn't watch this. This was all her fault. She shouldn't have run off to her aunt's house. She shouldn't have touched the dragon egg. She shouldn't have kept this secret so long . . .

Now there was nothing to do except watch the destruction.

As the dragon got closer to the town hall, something else flashed through the sky. Another of those winged demon creatures like the ones that robed illager had summoned? No, it was far too large for that. The figure looked human. And that human looked a lot like Aunt Meryl, her white puff of hair whipping violently in the wind as she approached at breakneck speed. She pulled up at the last possible moment, that winged cape of hers flaring out as she stepped gracefully upon the ground.

"Huh? What?" Zetta said, still breathless. She wasn't quite sure what she'd seen. "Elytra," she then whispered to herself, remembering what Ashton had written in his journal. Wings from the End cities. Whatever *those* were.

The look Aunt Meryl gave Zetta was sharp enough to cut a mile-long ravine into the desert. But she glared at her niece for only a moment, because the dragon was swooping down now, about to obliterate the vault. Aunt Meryl let out a screeching whistle at the dragon and then yelled some foreign words that sounded a lot like the scream of an enderman.

The dragon glanced over at Aunt Meryl, snorted, then pulled up at the last moment. It made another slow turn, but this time it started heading for Zetta.

Zetta moved to take off in a sprint, but Aunt Meryl grabbed her by the collar and pulled her back. "Hold your ground," she whispered. "Don't show the dragon fear."

Zetta's eyes grew large. How was she not supposed to show fear? She'd never been more afraid in her life. She stood there, shaking and quaking and about to vomit all over the place, but she held her ground. The dragon slitted its eyes at her again. It flew right over her head, and for a moment, it felt to Zetta like she was caught in a sandstorm.

Zetta held firm, though her legs wanted so badly to give out. Then, just when she thought it was over, the very tip of the dragon's tail came down and bopped her in the head. Gently, for a dragon.

She'd still have a headache for days.

The dragon landed on top of the rubble pile that used to be the belltower, perching there, wings still flapping. It stared at Aunt Meryl as she continued to speak to it in that scratchy, scraping language that had to be tearing up her throat. The dragon finally settled down, looking frustrated and a little ashamed.

"Care to explain why there's a nearly grown ender dragon in the middle of the town square?" Aunt Meryl said to Zetta.

"It was a series of very bad decisions," Zetta mumbled, much too shaken to say more than that.

"But she saved me!" Ashton said, running up behind them. "And the dragon did take out the last of the illager raid. Who knows what would have happened if it hadn't." The dragon's tail started twitching as Ashton got closer, as if there was just a bit of recognition still there, but even Ashton didn't dare look it in the eye. There was no way they could claim the dragon to be a friend anymore. Its destructive forces were leashed for now, but that could change at any moment.

"She saved the farm," Nana said. "Our entire crop could have been decimated if it weren't for Zetta coming back for us."

Papa stood firm beside his wife, still gripping a potato and giving the dragon major stink-eye. Rift and Rayne nodded. Slowly, other townspeople emerged from the vault. Most stood back, far away from the dragon, but Mayor Maxine approached.

"Zetta saved the town. Her ideas gave us a chance at defending ourselves." She looked at Zetta's father and nodded with that weird knowing look they always shared.

"Maybe magic does have a place in Sienna Dunes, Zetta," Father said, and though he spoke Zetta's name, he was looking right at his sister. "I was wrong. This town does have room for a potioner. Or two."

Aunt Meryl stiffened up, cleared her throat, and wiped at the corner of her eye. "Got sand in my eyes," she grunted. "And anyway, I've got to get this dragon back to where it belongs, which is definitely not here. Sienna Dunes is lucky the dragon hasn't gone through its final molting. The whole Overworld is lucky it hasn't gone through its final molting."

Aunt Meryl turned to leave. She put two fingers in her mouth to whistle to the dragon, but before she could, Zetta yelled, "Wait! Just a minute!"

Zetta ran to the tool shop and dug a stone shovel out of the inventory. She left a hastily scribbled IOU note on the counter of the shop, then ran over to Captain Zayden and whispered into his ear. It was time to call in her favor. He nodded, then took the shovel and scurried off.

"Thanks everyone, for the kind words, but I couldn't have done it without each and every one of you. We fended off this raid together. All of us." Zetta sighed. "But I also want to say sorry to everyone. To Dad, for hiding the truth from you. To Aunt Meryl, for destroying your potions and breaking your dragon egg."

"Don't forget about almost creating a wither!" Rift said, not being helpful as usual.

"Yeah, that too, I guess." Zetta shrugged. "Sorry to my friends for dragging you into my mess. And sorry the town is such a wreck now. But I promise I won't be going anywhere until every block has been replaced and every building has been fixed."

Captain Zayden came sprinting back with the shovel, now glowing purple with an enchantment. Everyone looked at it, amazed. "Mending, IV, just like you asked," he said, presenting the shovel to Zetta like she was being knighted.

Zetta thanked him quietly, then took the shovel. She pulled a piece of coal out of her pack, then drew eyes and a smiley mouth on the face of the shovel. It wouldn't replace Meechie, but with a high-level mending enchantment, hopefully the shovel would be able to repair itself and withstand the dragon's gnawing for a long, long time.

"Most of all, I want to say sorry to Dragon, for not believing in you." Zetta approached the dragon, just taking a few steps at first. When it saw the shiny shovel, the hostility seemed to drain out of its bones, so Zetta dared to get a little closer. "You are wonderful. I'm almost glad I broke your egg so I could get to know you." Zetta swallowed. "Almost."

She handed the shovel to Aunt Meryl. "We used this for—"

"You don't have to explain," Aunt Meryl said with a wink. "This isn't my first run-in with an ender dragon." She stashed the shovel away in her pack. "You did a fine job, Zetta. Considering. I hope you won't mind terribly if I ask you to keep checking on my place for a bit."

"Sure, definitely!" Zetta said, then looked at her father. "If that's okay?"

Father nodded, exasperated, but happy. "Founder's Day is next month," he said to his sister. "There's a spot for you at the table, if you want to come back and join us, Meryl."

"We'll see, Carl," Aunt Meryl said. "Maybe if I'm back by then."

"Back from where?" Ashton asked. He was worried about the dragon, even with all the destruction it had caused. Zetta felt that worry, too. Deep down, she didn't want to see the dragon go. She didn't want to give up on the idea that maybe, just maybe, it could be Sienna Dunes' ultimate protector. Maybe if they just trained it a little harder, the dragon could keep them all safe from any threat that might come for their town.

But as Zetta looked around at her friends and family and fellow townspeople, she saw that Sienna Dunes already had what it needed to keep itself safe. They would all come together as one, using their skills and love for one another to make sure their town thrived.

"Where? I think you know," Meryl said, winking at Ashton.

THE END

ACKNOWLEDGMENTS

I punched my first tree over three years ago now and still remember the stress I felt as night set in and I struggled to build my first dirt hut. I remember the exhilaration of mining my first diamond and the anguish of losing it shortly after when a skeleton shot me into a giant pool of lava. There have been many, many Minecraft adventures since, and I thank you, Dear Reader, for going on this one with me.

Getting to write in this universe has been a huge honor, and my heartfelt thanks goes out to the entire Minecraft community. Eternal thanks to the designers and developers who have bestowed us with this sandbox for our imaginations. Thanks to the YouTubers whose creativity and passion begets more of the same millions of times over. Thanks to the players who rock their Minecraft t-shirts and backpacks, spreading the word and bringing more into our fold. And thanks to the many countless others who work their brilliant magic behind the scenes. And last, but not least, a very special thanks to Mojang for entrusting me with this story, to Jennifer for potioning up this opportunity to tell it, and to all the Alexes who helped to make it shine.

I am so glad we get to share this world together.

ABOUT THE AUTHOR

NICKY DRAYDEN resides in Austin, Texas, where being weird is highly encouraged, if not required. Her other work includes *Overwatch: The Hero of Numbani*—a novel about the misadventures of a kid genius and her pet robot—as well as a collection of stories for Magic: The Gathering that dive deep into the megacity of Ravnica. Her adult works include *The Prey of Gods*, *Temper*, and the Escaping Exodus duology.

nickydrayden.com
Twitter: @nickydrayden

ABOUT THE TYPE

This book was set in Electra, a typeface designed for Linotype by W. A. Dwiggins, the renowned type designer (1880–1956). Electra is a fluid typeface, avoiding the contrasts of thick and thin strokes that are prevalent in most modern typefaces.

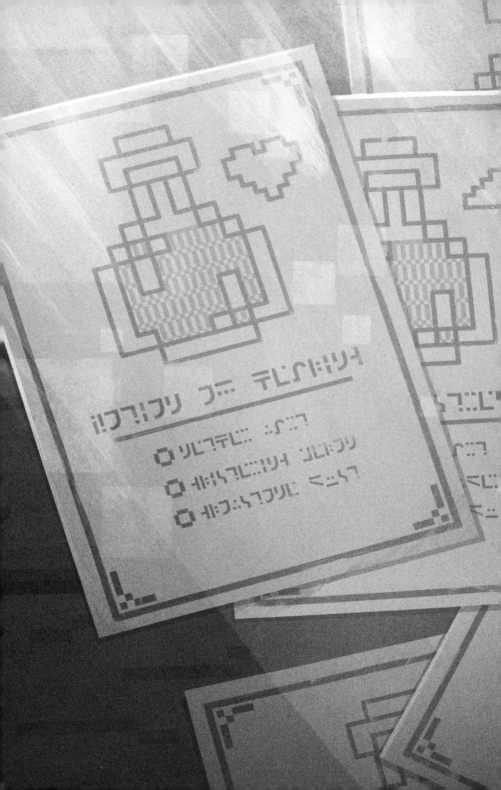